# SPY TRAP

The party couldn't be any nicer. Splendid music, limitless champagne, a perfectly beautiful hostess who was very friendly. A fine way to spend an evening. To Jim Phelps, chief agent of the Impossible Missions Force, it was a fine way to trap the double-agent who called himself Atlas.

The quarry was somewhere in the room, hidden behind a brilliant disguise. Yet Phelps knew Atlas would give himself away before the party's finish. He waited patiently.

Suddenly he felt the cold muzzle of a gun on the back of his neck. The waiting was over . . .

# MISSION: IMPOSSIBLE #2
# CODE NAME: JUDAS

■ ■ ■ BY MAX WALKER

POPULAR LIBRARY • NEW YORK

# CODE NAME: JUDAS

# CHAPTER 1

The message, when it arrived at the desk of the Paris Hilton where Jim Phelps was staying, was quite innocuous.

Phelps, a tall trimly-built American with prematurely gray hair, looked every inch the banking executive he was stated to be on his passport. He had chosen the Hilton, with its view of the Eiffel Tower, because the latest edition of *Fielding's Travel Guide to Europe* had assured him the lobby contained a stock ticker bringing the latest word from Wall Street. (Phelps made it a point to visit the ticker at least twice each day.)

As Jim Phelps studied the message, which informed him that the *machine dictographique* of M. Phelps had been repaired and could be picked up at the establishment of J. Massell at his convenience, he looked the very personification of the well-to-do Yankee tourist of the more sophisticated variety. Indeed, although he'd only been in Paris for twenty-four hours, he'd covered a good deal of ground. He'd eaten a gourmet meal at the Plaza-Athenée, ascended the elevator to the top of the Arc de Triomphe, fought two pitched battles with cab drivers and sampled the night action at *Le Drug Store* and *New Jimmy's*.

Phelps' single-breasted blue blazer with oversize brass buttons and pearl-gray trousers were well pressed and *right*. There were, however, several invisible differences. The heavy, gold buckle of Mr. Phelps' belt was in fact a single-shot, .22-caliber pistol; one brass button on his left sleeve contained a compact miniaturized "bug"; its counterpart on the right sleeve hid a needle impregnated in curare, for extreme emergencies.

Mr. James Phelps was not quite an ordinary man. He was a professional secret agent, trained and seasoned in all the modern techniques of espionage and sabotage. He was a member of an organization unknown to all but a handful of men —an organization whose very existence the United States Government denied: The Impossible Missions Force. Moreover, to the other members of the I.M.F.—all of whom were dedicated to performing secret operations designated by their shadowy superiors as "impossible" for any other group to perform—Jim Phelps was a mystery, a "faceless man" with no identity other than that he assumed on the missions he undertook.

Now, standing in the Paris Hilton lobby with the message in his hand, Phelps demonstrated that he was made of flesh and blood. He swore aloud. He'd just met in the coffee shop a charming and nobly proportioned Swedish girl and made a cocktail date for today with her. He was due to meet her in the lobby in exactly 33 minutes. That date must now be canceled.

Leaving a regretful note to Mlle. Bergquist with the message clerk, he stepped out into the noisy, orange-colored Parisian twilight. Dodging past Citröens and Renaults buzzing about him like angry bees, he threaded his way three blocks west to the modest establishment of J. Massell, whose small black sign hung in a single, dusty, plate-glass window read, *Réparations Électroniques*.

From the plywood partition between the front and rear of the store appeared a thin, hungry-looking man with a drooping mustache.

"M. Massell?" queried Jim Phelps. "I am M. Phelps. I've come for my machine."

"Ah, yes, M. Phelps," said the proprietor. "Yours is the Stenocord . . . but there is a little confusion."

"Oh."

"Two of the same machine were brought in the same day." The man waved one gaunt arm apologetically. "Can you describe some identifying mark on your machine?"

Phelps hesitated a moment. "Yes—there's a jagged scratch on the case, shaped like a 'W'."

"Quite so, sir," M. Massell nodded, "We must take these precautions to protect our . . . customers. Will you come this way to test the machine?"

Phelps followed the proprietor to a sound-proof booth where he was handed the compact dictating machine. "This is it, all right," he said. (A curious aspect of this transaction was that the case was absolutely free of scratches, W-shaped or otherwise.)

Inside the booth, Phelps ran his hands over every surface of the narrow enclosure to check for "bugs." Satisfied, he flipped the "on" button, and spoke into the microphone the words of the Gettysburg Address, followed by the lyrics of *April in Paris*. He then flipped the "playback" and listened with intense concentration to an entirely different voice speaking entirely different words:

"Good afternoon, Mr. Phelps. . . . An urgent matter has come to our attention—one that must be dealt with immediately. . . . The man whose code name is Atlas has operated for the past 15 years the largest and most effective free-lance spy ring in the world. Recently in the pay of the Russian K.G.B. he penetrated the inmost security of Red China and is known to have obtained complete details of Plan Z, the secret Chinese plan for nuclear development and war on the West, including Russia. The importance of this plan to all parties is tremendous. . . ."

Phelps peered out the glass-windowed booth, satisfied himself that the electronic repairman was busy in front of his shop, then returned his close attention to the recorded voice.

"The agent known as Atlas is—or was—a remarkable man. He has what is known as an *eidetic memory;* he is a veritable human computer and can store a multitude of facts and details. The full details of the Red Chinese Plan Z exist in only one place outside the impregnable government vaults of Peking—in the head of Atlas. . . . Only a month ago, for reasons unknown, Atlas broke contact with his Russian masters and fled China. He arrived in Geneva, Switzerland, carrying the passport of Efrem Olson, an American missionary to China; but mysterious forces, either Chinese or Russian, somehow managed to have the Swiss authorities lift his passport and hold him in 'protective custody.' Early this morning he eluded guards, rented a car and was killed eleven miles outside the city when his car went off the Lausanne Road. . . .

"The body has been amply identified. It fits exactly the photo and description on the passport with which Atlas entered Switzerland. It matches police records. And—one thing further—Atlas wore a prosthetic nose—his own was blown off during a sabotage incident in Hungary during World War II. . . ."

Jim Phelps took a moment, as the voice paused, to light a cigaret and check the security situation outside his booth. All was clear. The relentless voice resumed its drone:

"Nevertheless, there is reason to believe Atlas is alive and that his 'death' was staged to distract his pursuers and enable him to reach a sanctuary from which he can sell his secrets to the highest bidder. . . . If you accept the assignment, Phelps, your job is to go to Geneva, locate the 'dead' Atlas and bring him back alive to what we shall call 'friendly hands'. . . . As always if you or any of your I.M.

11

Force are caught or killed the Secretary will disavow any knowledge of your actions. You are absolutely on your own.

"One more thing: the man who gave you this stenographic machine will hand you, on your way out, a 'maintenance manual' for the same. Acceptance of the manual signifies acceptance of the job. This will contain photos and other important information which is to be burned after showing to your group. . . . This message is self-erasing; there is no need to destroy the tape. . . ."

Jim Phelps straightened his tie, stubbed out his cigaret and, Stenocord case in hand, walked out of the shop, wordlessly accepting the service manual handed him by the thin repair man with a "For M'sieu's convenience."

Jim Phelps' footsteps were jaunty as he headed back toward the tall column of the hotel, now glittering with a multitude of lights in the newborn darkness. Phelps always felt a sudden burst of exhilaration at a new assignment even when, as now, it interrupted the pleasures of the good life. As long as a man was in this game, there was always a certain build-up of tension waiting for the next job that was inevitably around the corner. Once the word came, there was a sense of release that was almost sensual.

Back at his hotel, Phelps locked the door of his room, drew the drapes and walked to the luggage rack. He opened an olive leather two-suiter and pressed his finger against the monogram in the lower left corner of the lining. It fell forward, revealing another lining beneath. Phelps took a retractable ball-point from his breast pocket, pushed down the button and traced the pen neatly along the outside of the lining. The pen's tip was specially treated with a diamond needle, instead of a standard point, and as it moved, it cut through a hyperresistant, thermalplastic shield. The second lining gave. Behind it was a black file case placed flush against the actual bottom of the suitcase.

Settling into a chair, Phelps opened the portfolio. Only a handful of people knew about the Impossible Missions Force; still fewer knew about the dossier: it held the only existing copy of every I.M. agent's dossier. Phelps had to choose four very special people from a very special group, the élite of espionage.

He glanced at three dossiers, but none of them struck him as precisely right. Then two more—not what he wanted. The next dossier bore the photograph of a handsome young Negro. Name: Barney Collier. He would do splendidly. Phelps flipped the dossier on the floor.

When he came to the picture of a man in whose face great strength was mixed with a strange gentleness, he smiled. Yes. Willy Armitage, second member of the team, whose dossier now joined Collier's.

The next few dossiers made him think of other towns, of other assignments. Still, he passed over the agents this time. Then came the photograph of a woman whose beauty would make any man pause. But she was Cinnamon Carter, and Phelps had professional reasons for lingering over the lovely features. The third dossier landed on the pile.

The final dossier contained the picture of a face that made you think you'd seen it before in a movie or on television—even if you hadn't. It was almost too striking, almost too theatrical. But Phelps *had* seen that face before, and he knew the man who wore it. Rollin Hand. The last dossier fell onto the pile. The I. M. team was complete.

Half an hour later, Phelps received a cable from his ostensible employer, an old, irreproachable New York banking firm, ordering him to Geneva to investigate certain new investment prospects.

There was also a wistful note from his shapely Swedish friend, Miss Bergquist:

Dear Jim:
Checking out this evening for other parts. Perhaps might have stayed longer if . . . Good Luck.
Lara Bergquist

Phelps read the note expressionlessly. Then he went downstairs and took the Metro to a cable office on the other side of town where he sent coded cables to the four he'd chosen to be members of this particular I.M.F. team. The messages, translated, summoned Cinnamon Carter, Rollin Hand, Barney Collier and Willy Armitage to a nine-o'clock rendezvous the following morning aboard a chartered boat leaving Dock 11, Quai Suisse, Geneva, Switzerland.

Next, Jim Phelps strolled five roundabout blocks,

then took a cab back to the Paris Hilton. By this time, it was 9:29 P.M. He cabled reservations in Geneva at the Mont-Blanc, booked passage by phone on the midnight Swissair flight from Orly Field, showered, shaved, dressed and lay on his bed to study the material contained inside the bogus Stenocord "service manual." The passport issued to "Efrem Olson" showed a hawk-nosed man with bright, slightly bugged eyes, thin lips, a square face and hair neither dark nor light. In proportion to the size of the head, the ears were extraordinarily small and close to the head. The passport described a man of 5'10" and 185 pounds, medium-brown hair, 41 years of age, unmarried, native American. The religion was Lutheran. His occupation was described as minister and his employer as Foreign Charities of Chicago, Inc.

The second exhibit was a blurred photograph which to Jim Phelps' trained eye had obviously been taken through a telescopic lens. It showed the naked chest and face of a man lying on a bed asleep. The face was unremarkable except for a grotesque cavity where a nose should have been; near the lower portion of the cavity were two small holes. The chest was broad and athletic and extremely hairy, with tufts growing out of the collar bone. A typed caption on the back explained: "This is the only existing true photograph of Atlas."

The third exhibit was a sheaf of excerpts from intelligence reports and memoranda, with several passages doubly underlined. Phelps took special note of one which read: ". . . In addition to his phenomenal memory, Atlas speaks unaccented English, French, German, Russian, Serbo-Croat, Spanish and seven Chinese dialects. He is skilled in all forms of combat, but because of a strong dislike of bodily contact prefers to kill with knife, gun or poison dart. The latter seems to be his favorite. . . ."

The fourth exhibit—and the last—was a photo and dossier of a black-haired man built like a fireplug with the flattened nose and scar-tissue-narrowed eyes of an ex-prizefighter. The report stated, in part: "His appearance is deceiving. . . . He is one of the brightest men in Koto-Yi, the Red Chinese counterespionage branch. Born of an English mother and Chinese father, he can pass as either an Asiatic or an Occidental. . . . He prefers to kill either with explosives or with his bare hands."

Jim Phelps sighed, put the papers in his carrying case with the special latch that destroyed the contents when tampered with. It was time to get to Orly Airport and the midnight plane to Geneva. He checked out of the Paris Hilton and got into a cab. As the cab pulled away, he was whistling *La Vie en Rose*.

A few blocks away, at just that moment, the lean electronic repairman, M. Massell, after working late on a stubborn hi-fi set, was locking his front door, empty lunch box in hand, when a battered VW bus pulled out of the adjoining alleyway. Two figures bundled up in raincoats, with rain hats pulled over their faces, got out of the bus and without a word thrust a cloth over the face of Massell. A moment later, his limp body was thrust into the cargo area of the bus, which then drove slowly away.

The moon, which had been half hiding under a cloud, went under completely. It started to rain.

# CHAPTER 2

The elderly English gentleman sitting next to Jim
Phelps lacked the legendary British reserve. He
used every trick in the book to get his laconic seat-
mate involved in a conversation. He tried dissect-
ing the French character:

"They really hate foreigners like us, y'know. But
lately, because they need all the francs they can get,
they're pretending to be more friendly. Don't you
think, old guy?"

Phelps smiled to himself at the misuse of the idi-
omatic American "guy," but pretended to be half
asleep. Then the old gentleman turned piercing
blue eyes on him and tried another ploy:

"Americans are the opposite. They pretend to
dislike foreigners, but actually they're wonderfully
warm hosts, y'know. . . ."

Flattery didn't get him anywhere. Phelps pretended to fall into a deep sleep, letting the old-timer

18

chatter on. At last, feeling a little guilty, Phelps feigned awakening five minutes before the plane was to touch down and listened politely to his companion's views on the Swiss national character.

"Industrious, but unimaginative," he said. "Now take this book." He tapped a copy of *Games People Play*, the well-known best-seller by a psychologist that described human behavior in terms of games. "No Swiss could have done it. It took an American to write this. Read it?"

Phelps had indeed read it; after all he was in the psychology business, in a way. But he nodded negatively, not wanting to expose himself to debate over the contents by the garrulous Briton.

At this point, the DC-9 landed and came to a full stop. There was much to-do on the old Englishman's part about unfastening the seatbelt and inquiring about his luggage. As Phelps started to disembark, the old gentleman seized him warmly.

"I say, why don't you take this book. I have another copy back home, and I certainly hope I won't have time to read it on holiday in Switzerland. Please do, old guy."

To avoid discussion, Phelps mumbled a polite, "Thanks a lot, most kind of you," grabbed the book and literally ran down the ramp. He had a big day tomorrow and he needed all the sleep he could get.

But Phelps soon discovered that speed was not of the essence in this Alpine paradise. At the customs desk he encountered the Swiss genius for red tape in all its glory. At least five multi-paged forms must be filled out in quintuplicate. The declaration of his luggage required an hour and involved six eager-beaver customs officials, each trying to outdo the other in nit-picking precision.

When finally it was all over, the mustached leader of the customs gnomes told Phelps with what sounded like surprise, "M'sieur is clean as a whistle."

Phelps ground his teeth and refrained from striking back with a much earthier Americanism.

Since a long night's sleep was now out of the question, he directed his cab driver to take the roundabout route for a night-owl view of the city. The navy-blue evening sky was shot with lights, and seemed much cleaner and clearer than that of Paris. Zooming along the broad, brightly lighted Rue de Ferney, Phelps saw the image of the city reflected up from the endless body of Lake Geneva.

Now they were swinging past the solid, glistening bulk of the *Palais des Nations*, lighted by a hundred spotlights—tomb of the deceased League of Nations and now European center of another generation's dream of peace, the U.N. Jim Phelps thought of his own mission in this city, smiled ruefully to himself and lighted a cigaret. He was borne at 65 m.p.h. past the spectacular *Jet d'Eau*, a column of water over 30 storys high rising magically from the Lake. Seconds later, he was deposited at his hotel.

The Mont-Blanc was one of the new, jet-age breed of hotel. Like its slightly larger neighbor, the Intercontinentale, it was a tall gleaming, no-nonsense shaft of structural steel and modern plumbing. The management of the Mont-Blanc had tried to soften the image by providing lakeside dancing and an *al fresco* grill, but the place still reminded

Phelps of models he'd seen of projected moonports.

Passing a bank of elevators on the way to his room, he thought he saw a vaguely familiar, stooped figure standing with a bellboy laden with luggage. He shrugged it off as he rocketed up to his quarters on the eleventh floor—a two-room suite with a miniature balcony overlooking Lake Geneva. He dismissed the bellboy, heeding Temple Fielding's admonition to overtip slightly the first time around to insure first-class service.

Sinking into a large armchair, he was suddenly aware of being very weary. He was also aware that he held in his hand the book given him by the talkative Englishman. He hefted it—the damned thing felt awfully heavy. A tickle of suspicion began working at a corner of his mind. He examined the book more closely, flipping the pages. Then, he ran trained fingers along the spine. *Eureka!*

Now all his senses were alert. He whipped out a special knife and slit the spine of the book; from it he gingerly extracted a long, slim object that resembled a ball-point pen. Tapping gingerly along the length of the tube, he located a joint and, in one stroke, severed the object in half.

Phelps had immediately recognized the tube as a "time pencil"—a form of bomb divided into two compartments, one containing a mixture of sugar and potassium chlorate, the other containing sulphuric acid. Once the acid had eaten through the barrier and combined with the other ingredients, Phelps estimated, the explosion would have been adequate to blow James Phelps and anyone else within fifteen feet to Kingdom Come.

*And he seemed like such a harmless old gent,* Phelps thought to himself as he cautiously dumped the potassium chlorate and sugar solution down the sink and flushed the acid down the toilet. *Or perhaps someone else planted the bomb on the old fellow.* The latter seemed unlikely. In any case, it seemed that somebody had penetrated Phelps' "cover." It was essential to track down the old man and find out who was pursuing Phelps and just how much this person or persons knew. The Atlas operation—and the very existence of the Impossible Missions Force—depended on it.

# CHAPTER 3

Eight-fifty-seven A.M., Dock 11, Quai Suisse. Lake Geneva was a pale-blue mirror stretching off into infinity beyond the early morning haze. An open, 18-foot, stern-drive motor boat lazed at the dock. A man in bright, tourist-colored shirt and porkpie hat slouched over the steering wheel. Visible in the seat next to him was a large picnic hamper and a gallon jug.

Eight-fifty-nine. A cab pulled up to the dock, disgorging a slender young Negro in a tan cord suit, carrying an oversize transistor radio. He climbed into the seat immediately behind the man in the porkpie hat, who hardly gave him a nod.

Nine exactly. A bus creaked to a stop just beyond the pier, while behind it a cab stopped. From the bus came a young man of massive build in striped shirt and black levis, carrying another picnic hamper. From the cab emerged a dapper man in ascot and hounds-tooth sport jacket carrying a wicker basket containing several bottles of wine. The two men joined their companions in the boat, exchanging quiet greetings. The man at the wheel of the boat looked at his watch now, for the first time, and shook his head.

Nine-oh-five. An especially ancient cab sputtered up to the dock and two elegant female legs emerged from the door, followed by a supple body encased in a short purple beach shift and a blonde head almost totally hidden by a large, floppy pink hat. The lady carried only a purse, a parasol and a fashion magazine.

Nine-oh-eight. The motor boat took off with a roar, with the lithe and lovely lady barely settled in her seat. Speed increased to 40 m.p.h. as the boat, like an impudent water bug, ruffled the serene surface of Lake Geneva. At a point about 300 or 350 yards off shore, the boat slowed abruptly to an idle.

"Well, fellow members, here we are again." For the first time, the blondish, rugged-faced man in the porkpie hat had deigned to turn around and survey the other people aboard. "Before we begin . . . Barney, will you do your chores."

The slender, keen-eyed Negro raised the antenna on his large portable radio and commenced moving it about over every surface of the boat, from stem to stern. For, indeed, the "radio" was in fact a highly sensitive detector for "bugs" and other electronic listening devices. And Barney Collier, who might well have been a druggist or an accountant on holiday, was in fact a highly trained scientist, skilled in theoretical and applied aspects of physics, electronic circuitry and computer technology. He was also, and not incidentally, a most valued member of the group known as the Impossible Missions Force.

"All clear," said Collier, retracting the antenna and settling back into his seat.

The man in the pilot's seat shoved the porkpie hat back on his head, revealing the clean-lined features of Jim Phelps, head of this I.M.F. operation.

"Gentlemen—and lady," said Phelps, spinning around in his seat to face them, "we have been handed a tough one this time." He proceeded to sketch swiftly, but in precise detail, the information he had received on the defection and "death" of the agent named Atlas.

"All right, we're supposed to find this *dead* agent alive somewhere in Geneva," said Cinnamon Carter, long slim hands toying with the handle of her parasol. "Let's assume for a moment that we can find him, even though he's a master of disguise in a city of disguises. But, Jim, how do we know your information is correct? How do we know the man without a nose who was found dead in the auto crash wasn't the real Atlas?"

Jim Phelps shrugged a solid pair of shoulders. "Some things we have to take on faith. . . . The words of my instructions, *verbatim*, were, 'there is reason to believe Atlas is alive.' Coming from this particular source, that's as close as you'll ever get to a flat statement of fact."

"So," added theatrically virile Rollin Hand, smoothing a crease in his sport jacket, "our first step may be roundabout—identify the corpse without a nose. It may well lead us to Atlas, and right now there seems to be no other route."

Phelps passed around to his colleagues the materials from the fake Stenocord service manual. The passport of Efrem Olson, missionary to China, through which Atlas escaped China and reached Switzerland, was studied closely. Equal attention was given to the fuzzy telephoto picture that was the only true likeness of the noseless spy named Atlas.

"Ugly devil," said massive Willy Armitage, a silent man not normally given to such exclamations.

"He may not be the next time you see him, Willy," warned Jim Phelps. "Remember, this fellow can put on anybody's face—and speak a half dozen languages like a native. When it comes to disguise, this guy Atlas may be the equal of even—Rollin Hand."

Hand, with the dignity of a great actor, made no reply. He merely buffed his fingernails on the lapel of his jacket to signal disbelief.

"And what about this other gruesome character," spoke up Barney Collier, who'd been examining the photo of the fireplug-shaped Red Chinese agent described as one of that nation's brightest counterespionage operatives. "How do we deal with him?"

"He's the other main entry against us in the race to catch Atlas," said Phelps. "We steer clear of Mr. X—unless, of course, he gets too close to the finish line. At this point, he doesn't even know we're in the race, and it's to our advantage to keep it that way up to the last possible moment."

Cinnamon Carter pushed the flopping pink hat back from her smooth white brow and fixed the attention of the group with her large, bright, oval eyes. She was a beautiful woman, with something of the élan of a countess—and some of the witchery of a great courtesan. (She had played both roles in her tour of duty on the Impossible Missions Force.) But she was much more than a glamorous woman; she had a keen, scalpel-sharp mind with the ability to ask the really hard questions when they had to be asked.

"All right, I've heard all the obstacles—and every one of them looks as big to me as Mont Blanc. What is our plan of operations? I can't conceive of one that can deal with all these problems."

"Right, Cinnamon," replied Jim Phelps. "This operation won't work unless it's broken down into at least four phases. . . ."

"O.K., Jim, let's hear 'em," said Willy Armitage. Despite his vast muscular bulk, seemingly immovable, the former Olympic weight-lifting champion liked action.

Phelps paused a moment to check the course of the motor boat, whose controls he had set to move in a slow circle about 300 yards off shore. Satisfied, he turned back to his colleagues.

"Phase One involves you, Rollin. Your job is to discover the true identity of the noseless man who died in the auto crash. The body is still in the

27

morgue, awaiting final identification. Your 'cover,' Rollin is that of Oscar Olson, cousin of the missionary Efrem Olson, whose passport Atlas used. Here are the necessary papers."

Phelps reached into the hamper next to him and pulled out a wax-paper-wrapped object that would have easily passed for a sandwich, and handed it to the ex-actor.

"Phase Two, Cinnamon, involves you and Barney. Your assignment is to attempt to flush out and identify the real Atlas. Somewhere in these intelligence reports, it is mentioned that Atlas, like some of his kind, enjoys night life, music and beautiful women. Of course, he does not drink, or else he would be dead, lo, these many years."

Phelps now looked Cinnamon straight in the eye. "Arrangements have been made, through certain channels, for the lovely and celebrated American café star Mabel Moon to make her first European appearance in the American Bar of the Hotel Mont-Blanc, where I am staying. Her accompanist —almost equally well known—is the brilliant Yankee musician, Barry Coker. . . ."

There was a shocked pause. Barney Collier was the first to speak. "Surely, Jim, I can't make this scene. I play a pretty fair fraternity-house piano, but. . . ."

"Have no fear," said Phelps, bowing in the direction of Cinnamon Carter. "The charm and beauty of Mabel Moon will make up for any musical deficiencies. And bring Atlas within reach of our net."

From the hamper, he drew out two more "sandwiches" and thrust them into the hands of Barney and Cinnamon. "Your credentials and marching orders are here. Please burn the latter after reading."

"All right, Jim, we'll go along," sighed Cinnamon, "but did it have to be *Mabel?*"

Unsmiling, Phelps turned to Willy Armitage. "Phase Three, Willy, calls for you to operate alone. As of now, you have been hired as a head porter at the Mont-Blanc. It appears that my 'cover' has been at least partially broken. It is essential that we locate and neutralize those people responsible for the explosive planted in the book, as described to you. I will be working with you indirectly, Willy, but I must lie low for a while. If I'm linked with the I.M.F. Atlas Project, the whole thing could go up in smoke."

Phelps, now obviously excited over the scheme, lighted a cigaret. "As a porter, you will have great mobility. You can move about among porters at the Mont-Blanc and the other big hotels—these men often hobnob together. Your specific job is to trace the old Englishman who gave me the exploding book, and through him to find any others who have cause to think James Phelps is something more than a Wall Street banker on a busman's holiday."

Even Willy Armitage's stolid face showed signs of excitement. "How will I contact you, Jim?"

"Not directly. Through the café singer Mabel Moon or her pianist, Mr. Coker. Like every other red-blooded tourist, I will come to hear and pay court to the charming lady. You, too, Rollin, as

Oscar Olson, will come to hear the new singer at the American Bar, and to cheer her in your rustic Midwestern way."

Willy received his package, and Phelps continued. "Phase Four brings the Impossible Missions team together. This is the trickiest part of all—getting Atlas, once caught, safely away from enemy agents and out of Geneva into 'friendly hands.' There are three alternate plans, one of which should fit any set of circumstances."

Phelps passed out envelopes to each member of the team. "Commit the contents to memory and burn the papers before we reach shore."

He scanned the faces of his four companions. "Any questions?"

"Yes, Jim." Barney Collier's eyes had the ghost of a twinkle. "Do you have any real sandwiches in that hamper?"

Even Phelps grinned at that. He dug down and started distributing from the bottom of his treasure box.

"Caviar and watercress—my favorite," cried Rollin Hand, with a dramatic flourish of his hand.

"Please pass the champagne," purred Cinnamon Carter.

Willy Armitage said nothing. He was deeply involved with *his* favorite—peanut butter and jelly on cracked wheat.

In the midst of the jollity, there was an inner seriousness—a knowledge that the new mission was now under way. And that one or perhaps all of them might never return.

Jim Phelps had one more warning as they headed

for shore. "Remember that Atlas is desperate, ruthless—a man of uncanny skill. He may be the hunted one moment, but in the next he may become the hunter. And he knows how to kill in a hundred ways. He is totally treacherous."

Cinnamon summed it up: "Code Name: Judas would be a better label."

From then on, in their own minds, the Impossible Missions Force dubbed their deadly target: CODE NAME: JUDAS.

# CHAPTER 4

"No, Herr Olson, the funeral director does not make any photographs of the deceased," said the big, husky *fräulein* with the carrot-red hair done in pigtails. "For this you must go to the Schweizer-polizei. I think that when there is an accident, such pictures are taken at the . . . scene."

Oscar Olson, a middle-aged man with rimless glasses, yellow hair turning gray at the sides and a doleful expression, scratched his head. Oscar, as played by Rollin Hand, was the perfect picture of a bereaved relative trying to do The Right Thing for a cousin he hadn't seen for years.

"Well, this really isn't in my line," said the imitation Oscar Olson. "But I promised the people back home—I suppose I better see the police and look at the grave. . . ."

He hesitated and looked soulfully into the blue eyes of the *fräulein* whose generous bosom was heaving sympathetically. "You—you wouldn't have the time to come along and help me with all these different languages?"

"Well, I would have to get the funeral director's permission. . . ." The *fräulein*, an attractive, not yet spinsterish thirty, was obviously in favor of the idea. Single American men—who being American must be rich—didn't come along every day.

From Rollin Hand's viewpoint, the company of a Swiss national would make his questions much more acceptable to the Swiss police. And doubtless the *fräulein*—she coyly informed him her name was Herta Himmelnacht—would have first rate connections at the cemetery.

The police officer who had investigated the accident that was fatal to the man bearing the identity of Efrem Olson was a stout, starchy man of thirty-five with a prematurely gray Prussian mustache. His first glance at "Oscar Olson" was frosty. But Inspector Summerlin unbent immediately when he saw the rosy face of Herta. After a brief, chummy conversation with the girl, he willingly opened the files on the case. Speaking in almost perfect English, he gave a crisp account of his investigation.

"You see, Ser, the face was badly smashed by the windscreen of the motorcar. . . ."

"Then how was my brother identified?"

"We are very thorough here, Ser. Within three hours of the accident, photos of Herr Olson's teeth were requested from Chicago by telephone—and received the following day."

"They matched?"

"Perfectly," said Inspector Summerlin. "In fact,

I have a copy-set of the photos taken by our medical examiner—of both the teeth and the fingerprints of the deceased man."

"And the prints of the man killed in the car are the same as those on my brother's passport?" anxiously asked the supposed Oscar Olson.

"Precisely," said the inspector, puffing with pride over the efficiency of his work. "As I say, I have this duplicate set of the photos—you may keep them if you wish."

"Oscar Olson" warmly thanked the policeman, accepted the offer of the photocopies and prepared to leave. The various winks, smiles and sighs exchanged between the dignified inspector and the buxom Herta didn't escape his notice. Quite evidently, thought Rollin Hand under his Oscar Olson mask, Herta was a most valuable aide-de-camp.

Then the fictitious Olson had an afterthought. "Oh, Inspector, there's one more favor I'd like to ask. You've been so good to me I hesitate—"

"Anything within reason, Ser," said the police officer, continuing to gaze affectionately at Herta Himmelnacht.

"The medical inspector who examined . . . the body. Would it be possible to see him? Your investigation is most convincing. But you can understand that the family of Efrem Olson still grasps at the small hope that this is some mistake, that he is still alive."

"We understand. Our Force is efficient, but understanding," said Inspector Summerlin, taking one eye off Herta and directing a sharp glance at the speaker. "Here is a card with the address of our

34

medical examiner, Herr Doktor Behn. He will, I'm sure, be agreeable to seeing you."

With a last wink between Herta and the inspector, "Olson" and his fair helper left the police station. Rollin Hand was now convinced beyond doubt of two things: 1. the corpse in the wrecked car was not Atlas, but the real Efrem Olson, from whom the spy had originally stolen the passport that got him into Switzerland; 2. the remains in the cemetery, even if he could get into the grave, would yield no useful information.

As he assisted the plump Herta, blushing pink from the attentions of the inspector, into a cab, Rollin Hand felt certain that if the photocopies matched those in the dossiers of the Impossible Missions Force, there would be no question that Atlas still lived and was, doubtless, somewhere in this city, hiding from his pursuers. It was also clear to Hand that the I.M. Force was still one step ahead of the Swiss authorities, who evidently believed that the late Efrem Olson and the super-spy Atlas were one and the same person.

And this led Rollin Hand to wonder: why hadn't Inspector Summerlin taken more interest in the person of "Oscar Olson?" He shrugged the question off. The wise thing to do now was to have a look at this police doctor, Behn, before making his report to Jim Phelps.

The doctor's office was in a tidy mews off the Boulevard de la Cluse, with geometric green hedges at each side of a white door marked in three languages: *Patients' Entrance*.

Met by a massive nurse, several inches higher and

broader than the sizable Herta, they were immediately taken to an inner room. The Inspector had phoned ahead, explained the nurse, and Herr Doktor was expecting them.

The doctor appeared, a compact, clean-shaven man with small eyes made smaller by the rimless pince-nez perched on the tip of his small, neat nose.

The fraudulent "Oscar Olson" commenced to explain his errand, the need of his family to know for certain that the dead man was indeed their dead relative, Efrem Olson. But Herr Doktor Behn seemed to be only half listening. He seemed instead to be looking out his window toward the Boulevard, his mind far away. After a long pause, he spoke.

"You don't look well, Herr Olson," he said. "You will please sit down in this chair." It was not a request, but an order.

He sat and the doctor felt for the pulse in his wrist.

"Olson" squirmed restlessly in the chair. "But Doctor, my health is of secondary—"

"Not good," interrupted the doctor. "Stay resting here a moment."

He arose and marched with military precision to the window. There was another long pause.

Herta tried to intervene with a series of her patented giggles and winks. "Herr Doktor, you are no doubt right about Mr. Olson being physically upset, but—"

"I cannot talk of the things he wants to know with the man in this condition," snapped Dr.

Behn. "My sacred professional oath would be broken."

Again he turned toward the window. Another lengthy pause. There was a noise in the anteroom outside. Simultaneously, Dr. Behn spun around and rushed toward the supposed Oscar Olson, brandishing his finger toward him accusingly.

Herta, screaming, was seized in a hammerlock by the massive nurse. Several helmeted heads appeared behind the struggling women—among them the gray-mustached Inspector Summerlin. In the same split second, Dr. Behn shouted at the top of his voice:

"And now, Mr. *Olson*, you will please *remove your nose!*"

# CHAPTER 5

Rollin Hand was used to the rough-and-tumble of undercover work. He didn't mind the violence of physical combat, as he'd proven on a score of occasions. He was a tough, case-hardened secret operative. But there was another side to Rollin Hand. He was a man of innate dignity and there was one thing he hated more than anything else: to be manhandled by a bunch of blue-clad buffoons in a precinct station. At this moment, handcuffed to a chair in Inspector Summerlin's office, his flesh was unhurt, but his pride was very much injured.

The meaning of the ambush in Dr. Behn's office was now clear. The police *had* discovered that the dead man in the motorcar was not Atlas. They had come to suspect, after "Oscar Olson" had paid his visit to the inspector, that *he* was the vanished Atlas. Why would Atlas expose himself so recklessly? It was difficult to imagine why. But perhaps the police were so desperate for a lead to Atlas' whereabouts that they were willing to explore the most far-fetched possibilities.

A series of almost painless tests on Oscar Olson's noble nose, performed with fussy exactitude by Dr. Behn, proved that Oscar Olson was not the spy Atlas, whoever else he might be. Now the supposed Oscar Olson was faced with the far more tricky job of convincing Inspector Summerlin that he was the real Oscar Olson.

"Now, Ser, now. . . ." harrumphed the inspector. His mustache quivered indignantly as he groped through a heap of papers on his desk.

The inspector was discomfited. He'd been wrong in his first intuition about Oscar Olson. He was in a highly embarrassing position professionally. The wrong identification of a man as Atlas could make him the laughing stock of the police force and could even lead to demotion. The only way he could get himself out of the hole was by proving that the man calling himself Olson was some sort of illicit masquerader—an enemy agent, perhaps a colleague of Atlas himself.

"The passport is in order, Ser," he huffed, avoiding the pleading tear-stained eyes of Herta, who sat in the chair next to the handcuffed prisoner. "However," he added, bunching his thick eyebrows together, "in view of what has taken place, we must hold you in custody until your identity has been confirmed by the U.S. Consul—and until other investigations have been made."

"This is impossible—I'll sue the police, the Swiss government. . . . I'll have you fired. . . . I'll—"

The fake Oscar Olson staged a brilliant tantrum in Inspector Summerlin's office, but the good officer was unmoved.

What to do? Rollin Hand knew that every minute was precious in this operation of the Impossible Missions Force. Overnight imprisonment could send the whole mission down the drain. A direct appeal to the U.S. authorities was useless, not to mention dangerous—the Impossible Missions Force didn't officially exist. A bribe? Hand was convinced of the absolute integrity of stiff-necked Inspector Summerlin. The risk wasn't worth the candle, as it was sure to enrage the inspector beyond all bounds. An escape from the prison? Out of the question, he knew, after looking over the stout bars of the windowless lockup. There was only one way out.

As Inspector Summerlin shouted into the phone at the U.S. Consulate switchboard operator, Rollin Hand dropped his head down upon his chest and placed his tongue beneath the topmost button of his suit jacket. A sticky substance adhered to his tongue. He swallowed it instantly, knowing it would be followed immediately by all the symptoms of a heart attack . . .

It came, exactly on schedule. Pains in the chest, a sudden tightening around the heart. Summerlin's face swimming crazily in front of him . . . a woman's low sob . . . a hum of voices . . . unconsciousness.

The distinctive hospital smell was missing, but the overstarched sheets and white metal bed indicated this was a hospital nonetheless. Opening his eyes wider, he scanned the small, scantily furnished room. There was a metal dresser, a bedside table, one small window, one door, one chair and in it— the faithful Herta Himmelnacht.

Seeing that he was conscious, she pressed his hand: "Oh, dear Herr Olson, are you better?"

He assured her he was, that he was subject occasionally to these small attacks—but they were nothing. He was perfectly able to get up. He must go now—where were his clothes?

"*Ach*, Herr Olson," said Herta, "zey have taken your clothes away—and a policeman is outside your door. You cannot go away!"

"But I must, Herta, somehow. My duty to my family . . . my late brother!" Rollin Hand put much emotion into the words of the false Oscar Olson.

Herta's plump, pretty face was a study in conflict. Like all good Swiss, she had an almost fanatical devotion to The Law. Like all good Swiss, she believed it her duty to report the smallest infraction to the Proper Authorities. Yet, Herta was one of those women who become bound to a man by misfortune, more surely than by love or desire. She and this nice American gentleman had known each other only briefly. But they had *suffered* together. Together, they had mourned the dead, faced the police, experienced a frightening illness. Herta was his, body and sweet, silly illogical soul. Rollin Hand knew this intuitively out of his vast experience with all kinds of women. He also knew that he must proceed carefully, or this loyalty could turn swiftly to venomous hate.

He squeezed her hand in return: "Dearest Herta, you must believe and trust me. I must get out of here *now*, and what I am going to do is not going to be strictly—legal. But it's in a good cause—and I can't do it without your help."

He gazed warmly and intently at her for a minute, to let the message sink in. Red-headed Herta gazed back fervently. She hadn't realized until now what lovely brown eyes Mr. Olson had!

"I shall have to escape in disguise. . . . There may be some violence, but I promise no one will be seriously hurt. I will need you to distract the police guard while I get away. Can I count on you?"

Herta's large eyes were frightened, but she pressed his hand firmly and nodded.

"Now you must tell me some things about my situation—"

Herta complied. The hospital was a small private one, a few doors away from Dr. Behn's office. The police doctor had attended him in Inspector Summerlin's office, and had said that he would look in on Mr. Olson again this afternoon. Meanwhile, Dr. Behn's nurse was overdue to administer some sort of medicine.

The situation was better than "Oscar Olson" could have asked. He set about preparing an ambush for the nurse. He explained to Herta that he would overpower the nurse and, since she was just about his size, put on her cap, dress and white shoes. While Herta was momentarily distracting the guard with some feminine wile, the "nurse" would bustle out the door without being too closely observed.

Minutes passed and the nurse didn't appear. The danger now increased that Dr. Behn and the woman would arrive almost simultaneously. In such case, the ambush would be doubly difficult, if not impossible. Moreover, the longer the delay, the more the likelihood that Herta would lose her nerve. Rollin Hand glanced at her sitting tensely beside him on the edge of the bed. He put a comforting arm around her shapely shoulders and felt a faint tremor ripple through her.

Another long wait. Then, finally, heavy footsteps and a woman's voice mingled with the deeper tones of the guard. The door opened just as "Mr. Olson" slipped under the sheets, and the nurse entered followed by a squat, powerfully built policeman. Rollin Hand silently prayed that the cop didn't remain in the room; if he did, the escape plan couldn't work. The man lingered a moment, evidently admiring the red pigtails and ample curves of Herta. When the nurse, who was rummaging in a black bag, shot him an unpleasant look, he stepped quickly outside and closed the door.

"I see our patient is awake," said the massively ugly nurse, approaching the bed with a bottle and spoon. "Now here is something—"

As she leaned over to give the dose, Hand with lightning quickness reached up and applied sudden strong pressure on the large veins on either side of the woman's neck. She flailed her arms a moment and opened her mouth to speak but nothing came out. Already her face was turning several shades of blue. She collapsed, all her vast weight landing directly on Hand.

Wriggling free, he ordered Herta in a whisper to remove the dress and white stockings. The girl was surprisingly quick. Within three minutes "Mr. Olson" was attired in white stockings, shoes and white coat-dress. Luckily, the real nurse wore her hair close-cropped, so that with the cap tilted over his eye and a blanket stuffed under his dress for padding, the imitation was fairly close to the real thing.

Now came the moment of reckoning. Giving Herta one last squeeze around the waist, he pushed her out the door in the direction of the guard and waited one split second.

"Ohhhh," he heard Herta wail, "I sink I have a run in my stocking."

This was his signal. He stepped boldly through the door, trying to mimic the nurse's overweight waddle. The policeman half looked up, jerked his head at the "nurse," but was obviously more preoccupied with the neatly turned ankle of Herta, who was going through the motions of giving first aid to a run with her lipstick.

"Good-day, nurse," he growled, none too fondly.

Rollin Hand, uneasy in his female garb, had reached the Boulevard de la Cluse and was looking for an alleyway to slip into when he was overtaken by a breathless Herta.

"Herr Olson, dear, you must pray for me. I hope I haven't committed a mortal sin," she gasped.

"Believe me, my little Herta," said Hand, looking nervously in both directions as he spoke. "No harm has been done. The nurse is revived by now, and none the worse for it. . . . But I must dash and—sadly—leave you for the present. . . ."

"And what if I'm accused as an accomplice?"

"I think if you explain to your friend Inspector Summerlin that the incident must have taken place *after* you left the hospital room—and that you're just as astonished as the guard to learn what happened . . . then I think the inspector will believe you and that will be the end of it."

Now Hand thought he saw the distant figure of the formidable Dr. Behn approaching.

"I must run now, Herta. But I shall see you very soon. And I shan't forget that your name—Himmelnacht—in English means 'heavenly night.'"

The fraudulent Oscar Olson kissed the girl and ran.

As for the girl, she stood stock-still and blushed.

# CHAPTER 6

Jim Phelps sat on the green esplanade running down from the terrace of the Hotel Mont-Blanc to the lake. He was doing his level best to concentrate on recent fluctuations of the *franc* as described in the *International Bankers' Newsletter* he held in his hand. But his mind was on other things. He was restless for news from his I.M. Force colleagues of progress in the search for Atlas. More than that, he was restless to get into action himself—something he could not do until the break in his "cover" had been found and neutralized.

Phelps sighed resignedly and put the *Newsletter* down on the bench beside him. He had with him also the day's mail and the three most recent issues of *Paris-Soir*. He picked up one of the latter, deciding to catch up on the news. He'd reached the third page of the issue of yesterday when a smallish item caught his eye. Under the headline, *Mort*

*Mysterieuse d'un Homme*, the story described the finding of the body of one Jacques Massell, owner of a small electronic repair shop, in a back alley the previous morning. There were signs that the man had been beaten, but death was not attributed to the beating, but to a fatal dose of curare.

J. Massell, *Réparations Électroniques*. Jim Phelps remembered him well—the thin, sad-eyed man with the drooping mustache who had served as the connecting link between the Impossible Missions Force and home base. Phelps said a brief prayer for all the J. Massells of the world—the errand boys and go-betweens in the secret war who do so well the small, inglorious but essential dog-work of espionage. So often, as now, they give up their lives rather than break the vow of secrecy.

Phelps now knew for certain how the Other Side had picked up his trail. He had been seen in contact with Massell, who had already been identified as an espionage "post office." Massell had been captured and beaten in an effort to find out Phelps' real mission. But Massell had kept silence to the end; of that Phelps was certain. The fact that he'd been able to inject himself with the curare that all I.M.F. agents carried on their persons was Phelps' assurance that his security hadn't been seriously compromised; the enemy guessed he might have some connection with Massell. Beyond that, they were only groping in the dark.

Jim Phelps scanned the scene around him. The esplanade was virtually deserted, except for a nanny wheeling a baby carriage some thirty yards away, going in the opposite direction. On his other side, about twenty yards distant, an overalled gardener struggled to start a rotary power lawn mower. Behind Phelps ran a five-foot-high fence of ornamental ironwork. The lawn beyond it, reaching up to the hotel terrace, was empty of people.

Phelps settled back to consider the evening ahead. It was to be the night of Mabel Moon's debut at the American Bar. It was also the night when all members of the I.M. Force would check in with their progress reports. Except for a distant view of Willy Armitage's broad shoulders among the porters in the Mont-Blanc lobby, he'd seen nothing of his I.M.F. mates since the meeting on the lake.

Phelps had many misgivings about this *Operation Judas*. The splitting-up of the I.M.F. team was, he felt, dangerous, though necessary. He had faith in each member's capabilities, but their true strength—and most of their experience—was in working as a unit. He had planned the final phase of the operation as a team effort. But now he was wondering whether that point would ever be reached. Was the "home base" wrong? Was the spy Atlas actually dead? Or, if alive, had he somehow managed to get out of Switzerland? A yes to any one of these questions would knock the whole I.M.F. venture into a cocked hat.

Meantime, with his group broken up in this manner, they were doubly vulnerable to being picked off, one by one, by the Other Side. Phelps thought for a moment of changing the signals, scratching the present set-up and tackling the various objectives via the group approach. But then he weighed the idea against Rule Three of his own personal rule book: Never scrap a plan until you have concrete evidence it isn't working—you may be succeeding to a greater degree than you realize. *Okay,* thought Phelps, *we'll stay as we are. But it sure makes me edgy.*

He took another scan of the landscape. The nanny wheeling the baby carriage was just about to disappear over a grassy hummock on the esplanade. He was left alone except for the gardener, still stooped over tinkering with his balky machine. A glance over his shoulder at the iron fence behind him showed him nothing but a wide stretch of vacant greenery. *It's the inaction that makes a guy jittery,* he reflected.

Going back to his musings about the problems of the current operation, Phelps got to thinking about the headaches of espionage and counterespionage that nobody ever considers—unless they're in the game themselves. They never write books, he thought, about all the endless waiting for a certain door to open, a certain name to appear, a certain face to pop up in a certain place. And they never say anything about all the treadmill activity, where you constantly move your feet without going anywhere. And what about the times when everything works, every tumbler clicks into place—and you open the vault and the thing you were sent after is gone and the vault is empty?

Sometimes he wished he were Rollin Hand, whose actor's ego became so involved in the role he was playing that he never found time to brood over the problems of the game. Or Barney Collier, who immersed himself in the mechanics and gadgetry, the "hardware" aspects of the job. Or Willy Armitage, who moved doggedly and single-mindedly toward whatever objective was assigned to him. Or Cinnamon Carter, who seemed to find enough satisfaction simply in being a lovely woman not to be troubled by the constant wear and tear on nerves and mind.

His reverie was interrupted by a loud racketing sound somewhere in front of him. Something plucked at his sleeve. Another of the same whined past his head. Bullets! But from where? He looked toward the elderly gardener, ducking low as he did. The machine was going—and it was clear that the bullets could only be coming from the exhaust chute of the mower.

There was no time to think. Calculating the angle of elevation of the weapon, which seemed to be some sort of machine gun concealed in the lawn-mower housing, he leaped to the top of the iron-work fence. The bullets spattered thick and fast, just inches below the soles of his shoes. Jim Phelps waited no longer; he tightroped his way along the fence for some twenty yards, then leaped for cover behind a clump of trees.

At this point, he noticed that the loud, rat-tatting sound of the lawn-mower gun had ceased. He pulled the concealed one-shot pistol from his belt and peered cautiously through the underbrush. The gardener and his lethal device had disappeared from sight. Phelps jumped the fence that had saved him and sprinted down toward the lake's edge. A few feet from the dike that protected the shore, he spied a long wooden shed. With a roar a small red Fiat

600 sedan emerged from the other end of the shed and rocketed off up a pathway in the general direction of the Hotel. Phelps raised his gun but decided to save the bullet—effective range was only 150 feet and the car was already twice that distance away.

In the gardener's shed, Jim Phelps found the weapon that had almost eliminated him—or rather the husk of it. The lawn mower was there, but merely the casing, handle and wheels. The lethal portion had gone, doubtless in the rear seat of the Fiat.

Phelps shrugged. A more exciting part of the game had begun. *Game.* He pondered the word a moment. He was beginning to get a most intriguing lead to the source of the would-be assassination by lawn mower. He headed back for the Mont-Blanc with newly purposeful stride.

# CHAPTER 7

Mabel Moon, celebrated American chanteuse, tapped her pretty foot in irritation. Everything was going wrong. The hotel management had assigned her a wholly unsatisfactory banquet room for rehearsal; the place was as big as an aerodrome and it warped her small, wistful voice into all sorts of strange shapes. Her accompanist, the famous Barry Coker, had just confessed to an inability to read music—and this had forced her to drop two numbers she'd counted on as the backbone of her act. Furthermore, the hotel *boutique* had shown her not a single gown suitable for her performance and she'd had to fall back on her own limited wardrobe. And, as a crowning frustration, they'd furnished a set of false eyelashes that simply would not stay on.

And then, complained Miss Moon to herself, there was that *impossible* man. His name was M. Fick; he was an employe of the hotel with some such title as Assistant to the Entertainment Manager. A muscular man with a hawk's face, he had what she thought of as hungry eyes. They wandered restlessly over everything, as though seeking to consume all. And, particularly, they wandered over Mabel Moon. He had hovered over her with pats, touches, squeezes, needless suggestions. And then, when he was really needed, when the air conditioning had broken down, he'd fled as if in panic. That was an hour ago, and he hadn't yet returned.

Like every true actress, Cinnamon Carter (alias Mabel Moon) had an intuitive knack for believing whatever role she played—in a sense *becoming* the character in the play. Just at the moment Mabel Moon was extremely annoyed at the low-voiced argument going on between the piano player, Barry Coker, and a certain powerfully built porter. Apparently it concerned the moving of the piano, which Barry was currently caressing. Meanwhile the real person, Cinnamon Carter, was fully aware that Barry Coker (actually Barney Collier) was receiving vital intelligence from his Impossible Missions Force partner, Willy Armitage.

And so, while Cinnamon Carter secretly cheered, Mabel threw back her lovely blonde head and let loose a tantrum that rocked the walls of the vast, barnlike banquet room. There was a five-minute delay while Miss Moon was soothed, during which the air conditioning came on with a blast of frosty air. Seconds later the oily M. Fick reappeared and applied his own kind of balm to the distressed lady's feelings.

Slight changes in temperature have a remarkable

effect on human events. In a short while, Mabel Moon was rehearsing happily to the spirited accompaniment of Mr. Barry Coker. Miss Moon was quite sure that she could scare up three suitable gowns for the opening of her act, and she was sure that her own eyelashes were more than enough for the occasion. M. Fick had settled back in a chair that gave his hyperactive eyes a favorable view of Miss Moon's undulating figure. And the heavy-muscled porter had left, satisfied with arrangements for the moving of the piano to the American Bar for tonight's performance.

Mabel Moon looked at the watch on her dressing-room table. Eight forty-five. Fifteen minutes to go before she was due on stage. Her make-up had been applied, every golden hair was in place. All that remained was to put on the metallic silver gown that hung in the corner.

The lithe, long-legged girl rose and paced about the room. She was no longer nervous, as she had been at the afternoon rehearsals. She knew she could do a job that would please the customers and satisfy M. Fick and his superiors. Now she was merely restless, eager for the show to go on. At the dressing-room door, she peered through the peep hole that gave her a partial view of the small stage and the area beyond. A five-piece band was grinding out a listless medley of Rodgers and Hart tunes. The name on the drum was Lester Leroy and His Yankee Serenaders. (Lester Leroy was actually a

Montenegrin and his sidemen consisted of three Swiss and one Spaniard.)

The bar itself and the stage area were covered by a huge red, white, and blue canopy. Out beyond the canopy stretched what seemed like an acre of dime-sized tables, now occupied by only a handful of couples. Miss Moon turned away and resumed her pacing.

There was a knock at the door. "Mabel, it's Barry."

Clutching her robe, she opened the door just enough to allow the slender piano player to slip into the dressing room.

"What's up, Barry? You interrupted my moment of meditation."

"Mabel, baby, I just wanted to give you a couple of suggestions on the 'Blue Skies' number. You're playing around with the melody too much. Barbra Streisand you ain't, y'know."

From the recesses of his black dinner jacket, Coker drew a crumpled piece of sheet music and thrust it into her hand.

"Good luck, baby. Kill the people." He patted her shoulder and was gone.

Mabel sat down at her dressing table and smoothed out the paper. In the margin were an innocuous series of scribbled notes. "Slow and easy here." "More *soul* in this word. " "Sing it straight." Cinnamon Carter's nimble mind swiftly translated these remarks into a report from Willy Armitage that her accompanist had received from the burly porter during the "argument" over the piano that afternoon. It was intended for transmission to Jim Phelps. Armitage had located the elderly Englishman who'd planted the bomb on Phelps. Until this morning he'd been staying in Room 403C in the Mont-Blanc. Now he'd checked out, sent his bags to the airport. He himself had rented a car—a red Fiat 600—and at this point Armitage had lost his trail. The old man's behavior had been most suspicious. Either he's a complete nut—or an extremely dangerous agent, concluded Willy.

"Mees Moon, you're on in three minutes." The bulging eye of M. Fick appeared at the peep hole.

"Ready when you are, B.C.," trilled Mabel nonchalantly, shivering slightly at the same moment, perhaps from the cold. Out on the stage Lester Leroy and His Yankee Serenaders had completed their final number and left the stage, which was now in darkness. Beyond the footlights, the tables were filling as if by magic; it looked to Mabel like a full house.

She studied the expanse of faces. There were several points of interest. In the second semicircle of tables sat Jim Phelps, the American banker. Within a few feet of Mr. Phelps sat a homespun-looking chap with a camera case slung over his shoulder—Rollin Hand, alias Oscar Olson of Duluth, Minnesota. He was in what seemed to be romantic conversation with a well-upholstered redhead in a bright-green sheath of clinging jersey. Mabel felt a small tingle of something she recognized as female jealousy, even though she had no designs on Rollin. *Stop being silly, Mabel,* she told herself; *in a few minutes you'll be the toast of the joint.*

56

At a table up front sat M. Fick with two other gentlemen. One was stocky and dark with a pushed-in face, the other tall and slender with silver-white hair. Presumably these were members of the Mont-Blanc management.

The oleaginous Fick got up from the management table and made his way to the stage. Stepping into the small spotlight, he launched into an introduction that endowed Mabel Moon with the vocal talent of Joan Sutherland, the charm of Edith Piaf, the beauty of Grace Kelly, the *charisma* of Jacqueline Kennedy. . . .

Knees shaking slightly, Mabel Moon slipped into her gown and stepped into the wings at stage right. Across from her, in the shadows at stage left, she saw Barry Coker. He winked and gave her a Churchillian victory signal.

Now the slender young Negro was at the piano, pounding out an up-tempo version of *Blue Moon*, the theme song. The girl star took a nervous look at Coker, who had seemingly forgotten all about Barney Collier, scientific prodigy and I.M.F. agent, and thrown himself completely into the *persona* of hot-shot jazz piano man.

As Coker breezed into the second chorus, Mabel Moon gritted her teeth and swept on stage and into the bright circle of the baby spotlight at stage center. The audience burst into a renewed wave of applause as the slender, undulating column of silver, topped by white-white skin and gold hair, slithered into view.

Without further introduction Barry shifted into low gear and Mabel, drawing a deep-breath, moved into *I Must Have That Man*. The voice, as projected over the excellent amplifying system, was small, a little timid, but with a pleasing huskiness and swing. To every male in the audience, and to every female, these were not merely words being mouthed by a mediocre girl singer. Every note carried the message: *this is a woman.*

The applause after her first number wasn't deafening, but it was quite satisfactory. With increased confidence, she tackled a fast-paced *Mame*, an excellent song for inexperienced songbirds since it was designed for no-voice actresses. A slow and moody rendition of *Solitude* found Mabel hitting her stride. As she took her bows after this number, she noted that the two cool cats sitting with M. Fick at the management table were applauding a bit after sitting on their hands throughout the first two songs. James Phelps, the international banker, was clapping vigorously and seemed well pleased. As for the tourist from the American Midwest, Mr. Oscar Olson, he was alternating between boisterous cheers and squeezes of his buxom redheaded playmate. Mabel slid smoothly into the lovely Beatles song, *Yesterday*, and wound up with a rousing *There's No Business Like Show Business*. The applause was enthusiastic, if not deafening, and Mabel Moon responded with an encore, singing a chorus of her *Blue Moon* theme.

Before she could reach her dressing room, a waiter intercepted her with a note from Mr. James Phelps, inviting her to join him at his table. There was also a note from M. Fick, congratulating her and inviting her to *his* table. Cinnamon Carter took

over the controls and decided that it would be politic for "Mabel" to see the management boys first.
She wanted a closer look at those two anyway—
there was something a little creepy about them. In
her dressing room she scrawled and dispatched
notes to Mr. Phelps and M. Fick, telling each she'd
be happy to accept his invitation in a few minutes.

"Ah, Miss Moon," breathed M. Fick, seizing her
hand and slathering it with kisses, "you were en-
chanting. You have won us all."

He turned to the two men standing beside him at
the table: "Let me introduce my boss, Mr. Jacques
Kramer." The blocky man with the pushed-in face
bowed and murmured an almost inaudible compliment in a toneless voice.

Fick then turned with a flourish to the tall, silver-
haired man. "And, the boss of us all, manager of
this great hotel, Mr. Erich Henreid."

The warmth with which Henreid took her hand
told Cinnamon: *this is a man who genuinely appre-
ciates women.* On her part, she had to admit she
found him attractive. He had the lean face, high
cheekbones and thin nose of an aristocrat. His eyes
were sea-blue and . . . then Cinnamon paused in
her thoughts, puzzled. There was something unex-
pected in those eyes. What was it?

She chatted for a few minutes with the three men,
sipping at the champagne Fick had ordered for her.
Both men spoke good English, the tough-looking
Kramer in a guttural gangster-voice, Henreid in a
liquid Viennese accent. Fick, however, did most of

the talking. How did Miss Moon like Geneva? Was her audience as hospitable as those in America? Was her champagne sufficiently cold?

Glancing in the direction of Mr. James Phelps' table, Miss Moon graciously excused herself. She left them, all on their feet bowing. Her last glance was into the eyes of the hotel manager, Mr. Henreid; she was still trying to read the message in those eyes.

Reaching Mr. Jim Phelps, the message in *his* eyes was all too clear. The American banker was impatient with the pretty singing lady. What the devil had taken her so long? She resolved to go all out to soothe the gentleman's feelings.

"Oh, M'sieu Phelps," she cooed, "I had zis terrible business appointment wiz my bosses to go through. An *artiste* nevair is able to get away from zese terrible people."

"Cool it with the fake French accent, Miss Mabel Moon," said Mr. Phelps. "As a banker who's investigated your credit rating, I know all about you—"

"Such as?"

"Real name: Mabel Jo Handwerker. Home: St. Joseph, Missouri. Father's occupation: tie salesman. . . . I could go on and on."

Miss Moon rose in anger, as if to leave. "Since nothing about me pleases you, Mr. Phelps, I—"

Mr. Phelps placed a gentle, restraining hand on the slender, elegant flipper of Miss Moon. "Dear lady, you please me excessively. I am, in fact, about to ask you to have a drink with me. But in my bankerly way I was simply attempting to establish a bridge between us. Perhaps my credit-check approach wasn't quite right?" "Well," pouted the trim blonde, "perhaps your intentions were good. . . ."

Moments later, Mabel was in the arms of the handsome banker, dancing to the strains of Lester Leroy and His Yankee Serenaders. Meantime her left hand, draped so innocuously over the shoulder of Mr. Phelps, was tapping out a coded message, transmitting the information received earlier from Barney Collier, alias Barry Coker.

Returning to Phelps's table, they were intercepted by an American flourishing a pen and an envelope; in a broad Midwestern accent, he identified himself as Oscar Olson of Minneapolis, Minnesota. He was an admirer of Miss Moon and would very much like her autograph.

Smiling, Miss Moon complied. She watched the sturdy tourist as he threaded his way triumphantly back to his buxom redheaded companion.

Just as Mr. Olson reached his table, two grim-faced men in dark suits appeared from the outer shadows and seized him in an iron grip.

Jim Phelps looked on in mild surprise. Mabel Moon quickly excused herself and hurried back toward her dressing room, Mr. Olson's ballpoint pen clutched in her hand.

As she reached the stage, a piercing scream rose over the strains of Lester Leroy and His Yankee Serenaders and soared into the night.

# CHAPTER 8

Jim Phelps needed all the iron control of a veteran secret agent not to rise as the men in dark suits seized "Oscar Olson." When a third man appeared and laid hands on the screaming redhead in the green dress, he moved forward—as any redblooded American banker would.

"What's this all about? What are you doing with these people?" Phelps thrust his way through the circle of onlookers and grasped the arm of one of the strangers.

"Police. Sergeant Immer," muttered the man. "We have here a warrant for the arrest of this man Olson. And for the girl."

From his breast pocket, he pulled out a paper covered with seals and official-looking signatures. Through his rimless glasses, Oscar Olson gazed dully at Phelps and shrugged.

"Please sir, you are an American," sobbed Herta. "Please help your countryman, Herr Olson."

"Well," said Phelps hesitantly, "it's really not my affair. . . . I can't interfere with a policeman doing his duty—"

"Please," implored Herta, struggling in the grip of her captor, "at least come to the station with us and be our—our spokesman."

Phelps hesitated a moment longer. It was essential that he not appear too eager. This was a tricky situation. He could easily blow his cover; that would be the end of everything.

At that second, there was a tug on his sleeve. He turned to face the slender Negro pianist, who thrust something into his hand. "You forgot this pen, mister. Mabel asked me to give it to you." Before Phelps could open his mouth, Coker was gone.

"You *must* come, sir," said Herta, pleading with her big blue eyes.

"I'll come," said Phelps, with the proper degree of reluctance. "But it looks like what you people need is a lawyer."

At this point, the plainclothesmen were growing impatient. They half dragged Olson and the redhead toward a waiting police van. James Phelps followed several paces behind.


Inspector Summerlin was extremely angry. He paced back and forth behind his desk, gray mustache quivering with emotion.

"Assault and battery. Evading arrest—I can charge you with . . ." he ended in a splutter of rage.

Oscar Olson sat slumped in a chair gazing

meekly through his thick lenses. The redheaded Herta Himmelnacht had regained her calm and was batting her eyelashes hopefully at the inspector. Phelps stood behind Olson's chair, looking as though he wished to be anywhere else but here—which was exactly the case.

"It is lucky for you, Ser, that the nurse isn't injured. Nevertheless, nevertheless, Ser, I'm going to . . . I'm going to . . ." He trailed off in another splutter.

When he had regained his breath, the inspector launched himself on the laws of Switzerland, the policeman's sacred duty, and so on, and on, and on. Midway through, it occurred to Jim Phelps that all of this was unnecessary. The only thing the good inspector had to do, if he wished, was to book the American offender and probably his redheaded friend. But obviously something was holding the policeman back.

As the inspector concluded his violent lecture, Herta perched on a corner of his desk, calling attention to a charmingly rounded thigh. The policeman gulped visibly and rolled his eyes toward the lady. Now Phelps saw the inspector's predicament: he was soft on Herta Himmelnacht. The last thing he wanted to do was place a criminal charge against her; yet she was clearly an accomplice.

Then another reason for the inspector's unwillingness to act came to the surface. If the case went to court, American consular authorities would become involved. There would be a lot of fuss—and questions would be asked by the inspector's superiors about how he had made it so easy for this silly

American to escape his custody. And this would revive Summerlin's error in mistaking Olson for the spy without a nose. Another embarrassment.

"Kind Inspector," said Herta. "May I speak to you a moment—in a private place?"

"I don't know, *Fräulein*," growled the inspector. "Your own part in this business is . . . is very irregular."

He paced a moment more and then took the girl brusquely by the arm and led her into an adjoining room, muttering, "It is very late for explanations, *Fräulein* Himmelnacht."

For ten minutes, the *fräulein's* whisperings and the inspector's grumblings could be heard. Then the door opened. Herta reappeared blushing prettily. The inspector still looked like a thundercloud, but some agreement seemed to have been reached.

The inspector cleared his throat and stared hard at Oscar Olson, who continued to sit gazing dumbly into space. "*Mister* Olson, this young lady has persuaded me that jail or a trial might be dangerous to your poor health. She has also convinced me that this incident was due to your upset over the death of a close relative—and that when it took place you were, in the legal sense, actually insane."

The inspector paused portentously. "For these reasons, and because I do not wish to create ill will between two great nations, I will let you go free." Another weighty pause. "But there are two conditions. The good woman you attacked must agree to drop her charges. And you must be out of this country within 48 hours."

For the first time since he'd been in the room,

Olson raised his eyes to the inspector. "I thank you, sir. I'll do anything at all, anything you ask." He removed his glasses and nervously wiped off the mist that had suddenly formed on them.

"If I'm not needed any more . . ." Jim Phelps started edging toward the outer door as the inspector urged him on with a curt nod of the head. The shapely Herta ignored him; she was happily clasping the hand of the rescued Oscar Olson.


*Forty-eight hours.* . . . Jim Phelps pondered as he rode the elevator toward his hotel suite. "Oscar Olson" was more or less off the hook, but he had created a new problem for the Impossible Missions Force. Either the whole Operation Judas had to be wrapped up within the two-day limit—or "Olson" had to vanish plausibly and Rollin Hand be resurrected. It was just one more damn problem at a time when the search for the spy named Atlas had hit a totally blank wall.

Reaching in his pocket, Phelps dredged up the pen passed to him by Barry Coker (otherwise Barney Collier). He recognized it as the pen Oscar Olson had handed Mabel Moon in order to get her autograph. It was a standard ballpoint job. Unscrewing the barrel, he drew forth a slip of paper covered with typewritten symbols—ampersands, dollar signs, quotation marks, and the like—from the top bank of a typewriter. Quickly Phelps decoded the message reporting Hand-Olson's adventures, then burned the paper until it was nothing but several flakes of gray ash settling near his feet. Hand's discoveries about the corpse in the wrecked car were useful, but only in a negative way. The man called Atlas was as far out of reach as ever.

He unlocked the door of his suite and entered to find a man standing on his balcony calmly gazing out over the city.

Phelps unclipped the one-shot gun from his belt buckle. The man, hearing his footsteps, turned slowly toward him. The stooped figure and aging face were familiar.

"Hello, old guy. Dreadfully sorry to intrude. But a very nice chambermaid thought an old party like me ought to have a place to sit down and wait for his friend."

"Back in the colonies we have a word for what you have, mister," said Jim Phelps flatly. "It's called *chutzpah*. Gall, in case you don't speak Arabic."

"I don't quite comprehend, laddie," said the elderly Briton, extending a trembling hand which Phelps ignored. "We had a nice chat on the plane and I thought we parted with good feelings."

"You left me with good feelings and a book that nearly blew me to Hades. And to top it off, you followed up by trying to cut me down with a loaded lawnmower."

"The book wasn't my doing, laddie. Somebody planted it on me—and I have a wee notion it was supposed to do me in."

"And what about all those bullets you pegged at me a little while ago?"

"Ah, that was another matter. I was in a sticky

spot. My people weren't sure of me—wanted me to take The Test. Go out and do us something, they said; show us you mean business."

With much difficulty he extracted a pack of Players from a vest pocket and lighted a cigaret. "I'm an old man. I've got palsy in these hands. But I'm still a dead-on shot with any kind of weapon you want to name, old guy."

"You came mighty close."

"How far away was I? Thirty yards? I *never* miss at that distance unless I want to."

"What's your name? What kind of an old man are you?"

"In our business the name doesn't really matter, does it, laddie?" The old fellow winked and tapped Phelps on the lapel. "I'm here because we can do each other some good."

Without expression, Phelps settled into a chair. He stopped himself from lighting a cigaret so as not to tip off any kind of reaction. The ancient undercover man continued.

"I don't know what your game is and I don't want to know. All I know about you is this: you're hooked up with a chappie in Paris who recently took a very long trip right after you visited him. And I know that the same people who gave him his ticket want to give you a bit of the same."

"And these 'people' put you onto me. How do I know you're not still running on the same track?"

"I'll show you something, lad." The old man unbuttoned his shirt, exposing a strip of bandage running from his breastbone to his shoulder. Peeling it back, he displayed a raw, red gouge. "That bullet just burned me. The next one is the finish."

"What can I do," said Phelps. "I'm not in the bodyguard racket."

"These people had an agreement with me. They didn't keep it. I'm out a packet. This is the thing, old guy: I want to do them in the eye and the best way I can think of is enlisting with you. Together, we can give 'em bloody what-for."

"Old-timer, you're still giving me nothing but moonbeams. Let me have something solid."

The aged one sat a short while puffing on his weed. Then he spoke, putting the words together slowly, as though each one was infinitely precious. "There's a man they're looking for. Even odds you're looking for him too. That's the job they hired me for. Sometimes takes an old dog to smell out the bird."

Phelps made no reply but continued to look straight into the old man's eyes.

"Am I interesting you? Let's assume I am," said the old man. "This chap they hired me to find, he's a dodgy one. But the old dog has found him. Not got him in hand, mind you. I can't take you right to his door. I have him pegged inside a very, very small circle, old guy."

Again, the codger paused. Patience was a weapon used by all agents; sometimes it was the most effective weapon of all. But Phelps was not to be moved. He kept his eyes locked with the old man's but said absolutely nothing.

"If you want proof, ask me something," said the old one.

"How can I ask you something if I don't know what you're talking about?" said Phelps smiling an open, friendly banker's smile at last.

"All right, let's suppose you're just what it says on your passport: James Phelps, American bank officer, here to do a spot of business for the home team. I still have something for you."

He rose shakily and walked again to the balcony, then back again. Next, he ran his hands with surprising swiftness under all the furniture in the room. Next, he inspected chandeliers, pictures, wall fixtures. Finally, he dusted his hands, sighed and resumed his seat across from Jim Phelps.

"There's a man who's come from a long way off —a very special man with very special information that everyone wants. The Yanks. The Russkis. The Red Chinks. Some people want it very bad."

The old fellow sank back, his face suddenly pale. Phelps thought for a moment he was going to faint. As an act of mercy he went to the liquor cabinet and poured two tumblers of straight brandy, handing one to the old man and sipping the other himself. His aged guest took a large gulp and seemed instantly to revive.

"That gash on my chest—can't cope the way I used to. . . . To go on about this certain man. He got the wind up in him. Wouldn't deal with anybody; scared they'd do him in. Went off and got himself killed in an auto smash. Or did he?"

The old man pulled once more at his brandy. "Answer: no, he didn't. It was all a show. Figured he'd get off somewhere and hide forever incognito. . . . I could have told him it wouldn't work."

Phelps lit up his best boyish smile. "And where do I come in on all this hocus-pocus and razmataz?"

"As a patriotic American citizen, wouldn't you do all you could to get him away from your country's enemies and into your own people's hands?"

"All right," said Phelps. "For the sake of argument, let's say I'd want to get this mystery man out of the grip of the Bad Guys. I suppose I'm as patriotic as the next slob."

"And wouldn't you want to see that the man who helped get him out—at risk of life and limb—got something out of it."

"Ahhh," said Phelps, leaning back in his chair. "Here comes the sales pitch at last. What do you want, old-timer?"

"Very little. A haven. I've had it in old Blighty. They're after me all over the bloody continent. I just want a billet in the states—and some kind of protection from them."

"Who am I—J. Edgar Hoover? I can't make you any commitments in behalf of the U.S. Government." Inwardly, Phelps felt the rising excitement of the hunter come suddenly upon the scent of his prey. Yet he must keep his cool, play to the hilt the part of James Phelps, private citizen. He must go on throwing every conceivable obstacle in front of the old man, while keeping him, unknowing, on a long leash.

"I don't know who you are, old guy. This I do

know: you're somebody fairly important. Just tell me you'll do your best for me and I'll take the rest on faith."

"Well-l-l." Phelps felt he'd now drawn the game out long enough, shown precisely the proper degree of reluctance and uncertainty. "I suppose I can promise you that if everything you say is true— if the U.S. really wants this character—this crazy, Ian Fleming–type spy—and if you can turn him over to our people—I can make you a promise to do my best for you."

"What you're saying, laddie, is, it's a promise. Right?"

"On my honor as a member of the Campfire Girls' Auxiliary." Phelps snapped a look at his watch. "Now, if we're going to do this thing, I want to get it over with as fast as possible. Can we go and get Super Spy now?"

"Not that easy, lad. We have to do a full circle. By now, they have me spotted. We have to lead 'em off the trail, ditch my car and then go for my man."

Phelps adjusted his tie, picked up a pack of cigarets and said, "I'm ready. Let's go."

One block down from the hotel, parked in a rear courtyard, was the old man's tiny red Fiat. With a cough and a wheeze, the car was off down the Rue de Lausanne, heading for the Old City.

Two cars back, keeping an even distance from them, was an unobtrusive blue Peugeot. The driver was slender with nervous hands; half his face was covered by a pair of oversize dark glasses. The man next to him, stocky and dark, also wore large

72

dark glasses. He was pulling on a pair of black gloves. On the seat next to him lay a machine pistol of German design and Russian manufacture.

His mouth opened like a trap and he said one word to the driver.

"NOW."

# CHAPTER 9

Phelps, out of the corner of one eye, was the first to see the blue car drawing up alongside them.

"Think of something, fast," he said. "Somebody wants to see us."

The old man gritted his teeth and downshifted with surprising speed. The needle on the speedometer dropped abruptly from 55 to 25 m.p.h., and the larger blue car momentarily overshot them.

"If you can't outspeed 'em, laddie, sometimes you can outcreep 'em." The old man spun the wheel left and sent the little car bumping over the curb and onto the embankment that lay between the highway and the glistening lake.

"Now the thing to do is find some tight places we can manage but they can't."

Phelps was craning his neck toward the rear window, watching for the blue death car. So far it was nowhere in sight. Meantime the ancient operative had found a paved bridle path, just a few feet from the lake's edge, twisting through a grove of pine trees whose branches brushed against either side of the car.

"See if you can spot a place where we can take cover and ditch the car, laddie," gritted the old-timer.

"I'm looking, but so far no luck," said Jim Phelps. "Anyway, you're doing 100 percent as a getaway jockey."

And, indeed, this man who had seemed so weak and shaky in Phelps' hotel room, was maneuvering the car with the skill and élan of a Jim Clark or a Mario Andretti.

"I used to do a spot of road racing," said the old fellow. "And besides, danger works on me like monkey glands. Rejuvenates, it does."

If danger was needed, there was a bonus supply up ahead, where the grove ended, leaving the tiny car exposed over a two-mile stretch where the bridal path wound through acres of treeless grass.

"Push it all you can, old-timer," said Jim Phelps. He thought he could make out, coming from the rear, a growing blue speck.

"I'm giving it everything I can, lad. But this is all you can get out of 600 cc's." The speedometer needle hovered between 55 and 60, but refused to go above.

Now Jim could make out the blue Peugeot in clear outline. Bullets commenced to whiz by the little red car as the pursuers drew closer. There was a sharp crack as one bullet smashed through the rear window and ricocheted around inside the car, narrowly missing Phelps' head. Up ahead about 100 yards was another grove of trees, but Jim wasn't willing to bet a plugged nickel they'd make it. He cursed the fact that all he had with him was his one-shot toy pistol. That one bullet must be saved for the ultimate emergency.

"Hold on, laddie, I'm going to try to trick 'em into the lake." By now the pursuing car wasn't more than fifty yards back and the bullets were bouncing off the little car like hailstones. Any moment one of them would hit the tiny rear engine or the tires—and that would be curtains.

Suddenly the old man wrenched the wheel violently and the Fiat whipped on two wheels into a tight circle. The bigger blue car roared by, brakes screaming. It stopped just a couple of feet short of the lake's edge, rear end swivelled around and nose pointing in the direction from which the car had just come.

Meantime the old man had gunned the nimble little red car up to peak speed while the pursuers were still backing off and swinging around to resume the chase.

"We've made it, lad, we've made it," shouted the old man as he aimed the car at a narrow gap in the pine grove just ahead. "Now you've got to find me a place to tuck away the car. This woods isn't very big, and they'll be after us in no time. Probably they'll be waiting on the other side."

But Phelps' keen eyes could find no break on either side of the bridle path. The trees grew together so closely that no more than a couple of feet separated any two tree trunks.

"We'll have to try something else, partner," said Jim Phelps. What it might be, his usually fertile mind couldn't imagine. Up ahead lay the end of the grove. And over the buzzing of their own small power plant, Phelps could hear the roar of the Peugeot, evidently circling around the grove to "meet them at the pass."

Just as their car emerged from the trees, the blue car came zooming at them from the left side, having circled the trees as Phelps had guessed.

"This may be it, laddie," gasped the old man, twisting the wheel so that their car went off the path and threaded dangerously close to the brink of the lake. At that moment, another flight of bullets struck. Phelps could duck, but the gallant old man kept his eyes at windshield level. Suddenly the old-timer groaned. A small hole appeared in his neck. He clutched the wheel still, but he was obviously in agony.

"This *is* it, laddie," he said through teeth clenched in pain. "Remember—I've narrowed the circle. Atlas is . . .where you are . . . office." The voice trailed off and the old man's hand fell from the wheel and his body slumped over against the door.

Jim Phelps grabbed for the wheel as the bullets kept coming. He felt one tire blow, and then suddenly the car was sailing through the air and sinking into the lake riddled with bullets.

Phelps knew before he hit the water that the old man was stone dead. He wasted no time in knocking out the already-shattered window on his side of the car and swimming out in the direction of the shore. There, under the dike supporting the bank, he found an overhang which hid him from the men in the Peugeot. There was a mass of fronds and underwater growths from which he selected a hollow-stemmed reed which served him as a breathing tube, enabling him to keep his head under water and out of sight.

The violent fall of the car into the depths of the lake had created a turbulence which so far had concealed Phelps' escape. However, he knew that in another few minutes, the waters would clear and his enemies would be able to see that the body of only one man was in the small car. Therefore, Jim knew he must make his way as quickly as possible down-lake, under the shelter of the overhang, until he reached some sheltered point at which he could steal ashore.

Slowly, gropingly, he made his way, hugging close to the bank. He still didn't dare raise his head out of the water and the limited supply of oxygen he was able to draw through the reed hindered his progress. His feet frequently tangled in the plants growing on the bottom; struggling to get loose taxed his air supply further. Once he tripped over a large hidden rock and sprawled full length. He was nearly out of breath when he finally made it back on his feet and got his makeshift snorkel in touch with the air again.

He had traveled about one hundred yards in this agonizing style—now he really knew what they meant by "a snail's pace"—when he reached a sharp bend in the shoreline. Once around the corner, he decided he must come out from under water and risk a look about him. He climbed over the lip of the dike and flattened himself in a clump of tall grass along the lake edge.

What he saw wasn't comforting. Less than fifty yards away stood the blue car, engine running. Phelps realized that he had dangerously overestimated his speed, a common phenomenon when man journeys under water. The driver, in large dark glasses, gun at ready, was seated at the wheel. The other man, a chunky fellow in black gloves carrying a wicked-looking machine pistol, was crawling along the shoreline, peering over the edge intently. Clearly, they had figured out Phelps' escape route. In another minute or two, they would be zeroing in on him.

He studied the terrain around him. The ground sloped sharply up from the lake to the highway, about 100 yards distant. Halfway up the slope was a scraggly patch of trees that would give him cover—if he ever reached them alive.

He looked in vain for some way to reach those trees undetected. Things look bad for our side, thought Jim Phelps. And then he thought of a line from his own private spy manual: *When everything else fails, run like hell*. He decided on a mildly sophisticated variation on the formula. Groping around in the tall grass that hid him, he located a round stone about the size of a silver dollar.

Squinting at his two enemies, he waited until both had their eyes on water's edge. Then he skied the stone in an arc over their heads. Simultaneously he took off on his desperate 100-yard dash. Halfway there, he heard the stone splash in the water and then the rumble of voices and the thumping of feet. He could only pray they were running toward the sound of the splash, not toward him.

The trees were only a few feet away when he heard a loud shout. Heart pounding, he dove for cover under the nearest pine. Looking behind him, Jim Phelps thanked his lucky stars. The two men were running back and forth along the bank close to where the stone had landed. *Home free*, thought Phelps, if only for a moment.

He started clambering swiftly toward the highway above. Already he was planning the next move. Piecing everything together, he thought it was now possible to meet head-on with the spy known as Atlas.

# CHAPTER 10

It was 4 P.M. The cocktail hour. And, appropriately, Mr. James Phelps, banker, sat in the English Lounge of the Hotel Mont-Blanc dressed in a $250 gray sharkskin suit, orange Countess Mara tie and $30 Bronzini silk shirt. He was nursing a *pernod*. He bore little resemblance to the bedraggled, soaking-wet fugitive James Phelps who had run in desperation for his life just two hours ago.

The new Mr. Phelps was expecting a lady; he had a cocktail date with the famous Mabel Moon. And, as he waited, he reviewed in his mind the progress of the I.M. Force's Operation Judas. Thus far, there was little concrete to show for all their efforts. And yet Jim Phelps' bones told him that things were moving.

The loss of the old man was a setback. He might have been able to lead them directly to Atlas. Well, that was so much water over the dam. Yet—

how had the old fellow put it?—*the circle had narrowed*. Phelps tried to recall the exact words the old man had used: "Atlas is . . . where you are . . . office." *Where you are* must mean that Atlas was somewhere in this hotel. And the meaning of *office?* There were, of course, business offices in the hotel. But, logically, the first choice had to be the hotel office itself.

In the elegant gloom near the entrance to the English Lounge he caught a flash of long, lissome, silken legs. In a moment the lovely Mabel Moon was at his side whispering a womanly apology for being so late in arriving. She was a smashing-looking creature in a psychedelically striped dress of red, white and blue. She wore silver, hoop earrings and her dead-white facial make-up set off her scarlet-red mouth and those remarkable eyes. Jim Phelps could tell just from looking at her that Cinnamon Carter sensed a new excitement in the air. She somehow knew that Operation Judas would now start down the home stretch, and there was an eagerness about her that she couldn't entirely hide.

Jim Phelps dismissed the lady's apologies, ordered her a *vermouth cassis Mont-Blanc* and tackled topic number one head-on.

"Miss Moon—Mabel—I think it's time you had a little party. Not a mob scene—just a get-together for the people who've made your show a success. The boys from the hotel management. Me, of course, as your number-one rooter. And Barry Coker. Anybody else you can think of?"

"Oh, I suppose I'll have to invite that awful Mr.

Fick, my so-called boss, with those dead-fish hands of his. And what about that American with the funny glasses—Mr. Olson?"

"I've an idea Mr. Olsen is keeping out of sight of the authorities for a while. . . . But Mr. Fick is a good idea. He could be a big help with something I have in mind."

"—And I really ought to invite the bandleader, Lester Leroy, and his silly little wife. In spite of his schmaltzy beat, he's quite a nice man and he'd help fill out the group."

Mabel Moon put one long slim hand to her hair and gazed into Mr. Phelps' eyes with her best dumb-blonde expression. "But, oh dear, Mr. Ph—*Jim*. I'm so helpless when it comes to making party arrangements. Do you think—would you mind . . . lending a hand?"

"Mabel, my dear, I've already done the spadework for you." Phelps reached into his breast pocket and produced a numbered list with such useful instructions as where to order flowers, how much champagne to order, what to instruct the bartender, and so on. This innocent list was also, of course, a coded message. It concerned certain operations to be performed *sub rosa* by Barry Coker, Willy Armitage and Miss Moon herself.

"Oh, Jim, you are a darling," cooed Mabel, daintily swallowing the last of her *cassis*. "Now, if you'll excuse me, I have so much to do. . . ."

The dapper banking executive rose and bowed to the lovely singing star. She moved sinuously out of the English Lounge amidst a forest of admiring eyes.

Jim Phelps smiled complacently and ordered another *pernod*. He was the perfect picture of a hard-drinking man of the world in meticulously planned pursuit of a beautiful, frivolous woman.

Mabel Moon sat at the dressing table in her bedroom putting the finishing touches on her face. Preparations for the party had gone smoothly. First, Barry Coker had come, ostensibly to discuss plans for music; actually, pursuant to Phelps' instructions, he had methodically disassembled the suite's thermostat, made certain adjustments, then reassembled it—while Mabel guarded the door. Next, Willy Armitage had arrived, wheeling a portable bar, and she had had time to slip him his instructions before the bartender arrived. Finally the musicians—a drummer, bassist and clarinetist from the Lester Leroy aggregation—had arrived with their instruments. Now they were tuning up in the next room, and it was past time for the guests to arrive. Mabel Moon, international chanteuse, gave her face one more critical glance and then floated into the living room, a vision in a short white brocaded gown with Oriental collar.

Barry Coker, slim and darkly handsome in a black tuxedo, arrived first with a "Hi, Mabel!" He positioned himself at one corner of the bar, bourbon and water in hand, where he could contemptuously watch the musical efforts of the Lester Leroy sidemen.

Next came the man Mabel hated, the creepy Mr. Fick of the wandering eyes and busy hands, dressed in a cheap-looking brown silk suit. He seized and embraced Miss Moon, with exclamations such as "My darling" and "My lovely one," and with difficulty she avoided his greedy kisses.

Behind him came the tall, aristocratic hotel manager, Mr. Henreid and his omnipresent sidekick, Mr. Kramer. The latter bowed stiffly and headed for the bar. Mr. Henreid, on the other hand, bent low over Mabel's hand and saluted her in the best old-world manner.

"Mr. Henreid," said Mabel, "it's so pleasant to meet a gentleman." She searched his eyes for the expression she'd seen the night of the debut at the American bar. But she could perceive nothing; they were opaque, neutral.

"Miss Moon," said Mr. Henreid, "I return the compliment by saying it is so rare one meets a lady these days." Rather hurriedly, she thought, he joined his colleague Kramer across the room. Perhaps her look into his eyes had been too searching, had warned him away from her. Perhaps, if he was with the Other Side, it had revealed too much of the woman who hid beneath the mask of Mabel Moon.

There was no more time to worry. Guests were now flocking in. The ardent American banker, James Phelps, gave a dazzling performance as a lover-in-waiting. "I kiss your hand, mam'selle," he said half jesting to counteract the fact that his hand-kissing technique was several cuts below the continental standard set by the tall Mr. Henreid. Staring about him at the other men in the room with the combative jealousy of the American male-on-the-make, Mr. Phelps tried to hold Miss Moon's attention with a series of rather blue jokes and an urgent dinner invitation. But the graceful vocalist skilfully outmaneuvered him. "You sit down, right on this couch, and don't go 'way. I have to do some more hostessing, but I'll be right back."

Two pretty, rather full-fleshed young blondes had now arrived, chirping merrily. They identified themselves as members of the hotel management staff. One of them immediately started dancing with Barry Coker. The other plumped herself down next to Mr. Phelps, who seemed to be getting slightly tipsy, and who found her company quite stimulating. Presently, they were chatting like old friends, and Mr. Phelps—his Mabel momentarily forgotten—had managed to work his arm all the way around his blonde chum's waist.

"Lester Leroy! My favorite Yankee from Montenegro!" Mabel excused herself from a conversation with the hard-breathing Mr. Fick and rushed to the door to greet the bandleader and his wife. Leroy, a small man with a thin body and incongruously round and jolly face, hugged Mabel with boyish gusto. Mr. Leroy's wife, a handsome woman with jet-black, waist-long hair and an abundance of curves, some of which were trying to escape from her low-cut red gown, smiled weakly at Miss Moon.

Mabel knew she was no favorite of Nadja Leroy's. But she knew just how to make the black-haired beauty enjoy a party. She towed her over to where Erich Henreid, the aristocratic hotel manager, stood, momentarily alone. Within seconds, they were dancing together, a handsome couple. Nadja Leroy's day had been made.

After one quick dance with Lester Leroy, Mabel Moon decided it was time to reclaim her wandering admirer, Mr. Phelps, who was showing a trifle too much enthusiasm for the teen-age blonde next to him on the couch. "Jim, dear," said Mabel in honeyed tones, "aren't you going to ask little Mabel to dance."

Mumbling an excuse to his little companion, Phelps lurched awkwardly to his feet and led Mabel somewhat unsteadily toward the dancing area. Clutching her around the waist, he guided her into a half-tempo fox trot.

"Mr. Phelps, your drunk act is frighteningly realistic," she whispered in his ear.

"Miss Moon, basically I'm a Method actor. I *live* my parts," he muttered tipsily. And he added, in a quite different voice, "I'll be ready when the action starts. Tell Barry to push the button."

Mabel Moon's next dance was with Barry Coker. A series of well-camouflaged taps on the shoulder gave him the message from Jim Phelps. Forty seconds after the dance number ended, the slender young Negro pianist was leaning nonchalantly against the wall, inches from the thermostat.

Sixty seconds later, the party began to warm up. In fact, everybody began to sweat profusely. Several ladies were forced to retire to the bedroom to repair their makeup. Mr. Kramer and then the manager, Mr. Henreid, tinkered unsuccessfully with the thermostat. Mr. Fick ran about rather frantically, accomplishing nothing, wiping his brow repeatedly with a flamboyant chartreuse handkerchief. Finally, Mr. Kramer got on the phone and commenced shouting in a mixture of German and French at somebody in the maintenance department.

The only person who seemed unruffled by the unpleasant weather conditions was the American banker, Mr. Phelps. Jolly, and perhaps slightly intoxicated, he moved about the room conversing with everyone who would lend him an ear. To Mr. Henreid he gave the unwelcome suggestion that any good American heating engineer could put things right in a jiffy. To Mr. Kramer he suggested that the hotel management ought to supply Miss Moon—and the party—with another suite, instantly.

To Mrs. Lester Leroy, chatting with a fascinated Mr. Fick, Mr. Phelps mumbled, "D'anybody ever tell you you looked like Jacqueline Kennedy?"

Drawing the oily entertainment manager to one side, he said, "Y'know, Mr. Fick, maybe you should have given this party in the bar where Miss Moon sings. Outdoors, y'know." He pulled out a handkerchief and wiped his brow. "It's so hot in here everybody's sweating as if they were in a sauna bath."

Mr. Fick seemed reluctant to continue the conversation. In fact, he presented a number of urgent reasons why he must leave this charming party at once. But the relentless guest, Mr. Phelps, clung to his arm and ignored his protestations.

By now, the crowd had thinned out. Some had left and others had stepped into the hall to cool themselves. Phelps and Fick were now standing alone in one corner of the room.

"This'll interest you, Mr. Fick," rambled Jim Phelps. "Science can do some amazing things. I have a friend, lost an arm in an industrial accident. Gave him an arm that looks *real*—fingers move, everything."

Phelps stabbed his forefinger toward Fick in emphasis. "Only one thing they couldn't do with this fellow's artificial arm, Mr. Fick. They couldn't give him an arm that would *sweat*."

Phelps fixed the entertainment manager with a steely eye. "Your nose is the only human thing in this room that isn't sweating. . . . Take off your nose—Atlas!"

# CHAPTER 11

Fick's eyes showed only a flicker of surprise. Then they resumed their perpetual roaming around the room. "I see the men have come to repair the thermostat—adding another element of confusion. The party seems to be temporarily suspended," said Mr. Fick.

Phelps said nothing. He waited, poised inwardly, ready for almost anything to happen.

"I tell you what," said Fick. "I don't understand what you are talking about, but you seem to have something—a business matter—you want to talk about. I know a much more suitable place to negotiate."

"O.K. by me," said Phelps. "Lead me to it. My business is talking to people. I'll talk to anybody, anywhere."

Mabel and Barry Coker weren't in sight as he

followed Fick to the elevator. This was a bad break; if anything went wrong, nobody'd be able to trace him. But this deal was too important to miss. Jim Phelps was only a breath away from his objective. He quickened his stride, following the solidly built figure of Fick down the corridor.

The elevator carried them nonstop to the basement. Mr. Fick produced a bunch of keys and opened a door marked "Health Club." "This room is empty at this time of day. Europeans have taken to your decadent American cocktail-hour habits. The only exercise anyone takes in the evening is the, how do you say it, lifting of the elbow."

"I read somewhere that the cocktail hour was invented by a Cossack liquor dealer who found himself with a surplus of vodka." Phelps chose to keep a certain thickness in his voice; if Atlas thought his opponent was slightly under the weather, he'd be more likely to let his guard down.

Atlas prowled restlessly about the room. The floor was littered with every conceivable kind of exercise equipment—mechanical horses, rowing machines, parallel bars, exercycles, exercise mats. A trapeze hung from the middle of the big, high-ceilinged room. Arrayed on a rack in one corner were a set of weights and next to them a half dozen pairs of Indian clubs. Another rack held fencing foils. Atlas, or Fick as he currently called himself, settled down on the floor, leaning up against the iron base of a set of parallel bars. From an inside pocket, he produced a pack of *Gauloises*, offered one to Phelps who shook his head in refusal, lit up and watched the smoke rings drifting upward. There was another silence of more than five minutes, and then the mystery man spoke.

"Mr. . . . Phelps. You have made a curious request. I don't know who you are, or where you have found your strange ideas. My name is Fick —Adolf Ladislas Fick. I was born in Austria of an Austrian father and a Hungarian mother. I have spent my whole life working in the world of entertainment—circuses, casinos, nightclubs, motion pictures. Once I was an actor. But certain injuries in an auto accident made it impossible for me to continue. So here I am, entertainment manager of the Mont-Blanc Hotel. . . . And here you are, harassing a man whose only wish is to make an honest living in his own way. I ask you, Mr. Phelps, is this fair or just? You seem like a decent sort of man, but you have made some sort of serious mistake. Now let's forget all of this. I will leave and go about my business . . . and you will go about yours, whatever it is."

"Mr. *Fick*, come now. I may be an American, but I wasn't born yesterday." Phelps sat down on the floor facing the other man, his back leaning against a rolled-up mat. "If all you say were true, why would you agree to talk with me at all? Why wouldn't you either punch me in the nose . . . or call the police?"

"My dear Phelps, no man's past is flawless," said Fick, sending another plume of smoke curling upward. "There have been, I admit, certain small encounters with the police—not here, in other countries. I prefer, if avoidable, not to make a row of this. Trouble with you could lead to trouble in my job. . . . But be sure of this: I will not be end-lessly patient. Press me too hard and I will take . . . *action*."

Phelps shook his head. "I won't buy it, Mr. At-las. I repeat the invitation I offered you upstairs: take off your nose. Or, simpler, admit your iden-tity and put yourself in my custody."

"You like to play games, Mr. Phelps." Atlas-Fick stomped out his cigaret butt. "I'll play games with you. Let's make believe that I'm the person you're describing. Let's accept that absurd premise. Just what could you and your government offer such a man?"

"Freedom. Safety. A chance to make a new life. Immunity from prosecution—and, above all, from persecution."

"Freedom is a delusion. Safety is a snare. There is no possibility of a new life for a man such as you describe. What you're trying to peddle are childish illusions."

"You're very wrong. But let's grant that even freedom and safety are relative terms. No man is ever 100 percent safe; he may die tomorrow under the wheels of an automobile. But certainly, our hypothetical super spy is aware that he'd be far safer on the other side of the ocean, away from the intrigues of the men who want him dead at any cost."

"No, Mr. Phelps. I think that your super spy, whoever he might be, would think differently. Like a rabbit, pursued all his life by dogs, he would be safer in the fields of his youth, where he knows every nook-and-cranny hiding place. Where he knows every trick and every quirk of the animals who are chasing him. Lure him to another place, and he would be easy prey. If nothing else, he might well die of loneliness."

It was Phelps' turn to get up and pace around the lofty room. Moving around gave him a chance to plan his next move without, he hoped, creating too much suspicion in the man seated on the floor, chain-smoking French cigarettes. Obviously, thought Jim Phelps, I've given him something to think about. Persuading him to come over to our side, of course, is something else. It still might well get down to a grim physical struggle.

And Phelps was too realistic to kid himself: the fight could go either way. Phelps was a tough, rugged man in a fight, trained to the teeth in modern techniques of man-to-man combat. But, he knew Atlas' dossier by heart: this man was not merely a super spy but a super-killer, of incredible strength and ruthlessness. And if Atlas came up the winner, it would be *kaput* for James Phelps—and for the I.M.F. mission.

As he circled the room, Phelps sized up the available armament. He had his one-shot pistol, but Atlas was doubtless armed with something equally lethal, probably more so. Indian clubs and parallel bars hardly made suitable weapons. As for the foils, Phelps hoped it wouldn't get to that—he'd gone out for saber one year in college, had made the team, but without distinction.

Presently, he sat down again facing Atlas, who seemed to be lost in thought. At last, the man raised his head and looked Jim Phelps directly in the eye.

"You know, Mr. Phelps, I am rather sorry for you. The people you are contending with for this fellow Atlas—I know a little about them. They are so much wiser, so much more deadly—and they pay so much better. Believe me, they will run rings about you."

Phelps raised his eyebrows but decided it was politic to say nothing. There was more to be gained by listening silently.

Atlas continued: "There is a man right here in Geneva, now, who thinks he is going to capture and kill Atlas. That's what he *thinks*. But Atlas has escaped these people before. In the end, as always, they will tire of the chase. And then they will come through with the money—at least a million dollars."

Now Phelps had to break in: "But what they're buying is all in Atlas' head. The only way their investment will be safe is if the spy is six feet under the ground. Talk about illusions: Atlas is only fooling himself if he thinks that way. The money will merely be bait for the trap that will eventually swallow him up."

"No, it will be an unbreakable employment contract—the employers will not only be buying Atlas' silence on the China matter. They will have the services of the premier secret agent of the world."

Though the man facing him was all but acknowledging that he was the legendary Atlas, they continued to speak of Atlas in the third person. It made Phelps feel like an Indian chief in an old Western film. But if that was the way his boy wanted it, that was O.K. by Jim Phelps.

"Let me tell you a story about a man I met the other day," said Phelps. "This old fellow thought he could work with the people you're talking about too. He was a clever old fellow. But he couldn't do business with them and now he's dead."

"I think I know the case you're talking about," said Atlas. "Forgive me, but it's an entirely different case. The old man was a fool. First, he had nothing valuable to sell. Second, he didn't deliver the goods he was paid to deliver. And third, he made a serious error—trying to sign up with the Other Side, meaning you."

"These people can't be trusted, and the old man's story proves it. That's the important thing to keep in mind." Phelps, sensing that the pow-wow was reaching an impasse, reached down and loosened his belt, at the same time palming the miniature belt-buckle gun.

"Phelps, *nobody* can be trusted." Atlas showed his teeth in a strange, skeleton-like smile. "The people to be trusted least are those who talk about how untrustworthy other people are."

"That puts you in my camp," said Phelps. Now he realized that they were merely marking time, like two boxers dancing around each other, looking for an opening. Phelps realized that a certain advantage lay with the man who made the first move. But he waited, hoping that a break would come that would make mortal combat unnecessary. Phelps was up against a man formidable in himself; and there was another handicap—Jim had to bring his man in alive to fulfill his mission. Atlas faced no such restriction: he could go all out for the kill.

Atlas put out his cigaret and arose. Both men knew that it was a signal. Phelps decided to try one more form of persuasion.

"I have a gun in my hand, Atlas. Don't consider trying to fight your way out of this. You're in a cul-de-sac. Settle now and save yourself a hole in the head."

The man facing him was now coiled, like a powerful steel spring. Phelps could see the heavy chest and arm muscles bunching under the jacket. Then they relaxed, and Atlas raised one hand tentatively to his face.

"You wanted to see Atlas with his nose removed. Here's your last and one-and-only chance." There was a faint ripping noise and the man before him stood, revealing a grotesque parody of a face, with a deep pit between the eyes. And suddenly the man's right hand whipped up and toward Phelps; something buzzed by his ear.

Darts, thought Phelps; he had them hidden in the fake nose. Flinging up his right hand, Jim stopped one of the feathered shafts with the small gun in his palm. The next move was Jim's: Atlas had clearly run out of darts. He swung the gun in line with the man's leg, trying to disable him. But the gun jammed, apparently disabled by the dart which had struck it.

Atlas leaped toward a corner of the room and instantly Phelps was dodging a cannonade of Indian clubs. The first three missed; the fourth knocked his feet from under him. Then Atlas was on top of him, grinning with that unearthly face and pounding at his head with another of the clubs. The first blow missed as Phelps wriggled clear. Then, swinging from the heels, Atlas brought the club crashing down upon his head. There was no time to get out of the way; all Phelps could do was throw up his left arm. The blow jolted him all the way up the arm, numbing it totally.

The force of his swing had carried Atlas beyond his target. Phelps scrambled to his feet and using his one good arm, flipped Atlas over his back. It was a good throw, but unluckily the noseless spy landed on one of the exercise mats and was swiftly back on his feet, charging the partly disabled Phelps. This time Jim met him with a right hook flush on the chops. Atlas fell back, half stunned. Jim Phelps dodged around him trying for a *savate* kick, but his limp arm slowed him enough that Atlas had time to get on his feet, wielding an Indian club he had retrieved from the floor.

Phelps backed off toward the Indian-club rack; this time he was ready, armed with one of the stumpy wooden clubs. Like seventeenth-century duelists, they moved back and forth across the floor, striking and parrying, with neither man gaining the advantage. Being essentially a one-handed form of combat, it did give Jim Phelps' damaged arm a chance to recover; he could detect a faint tingle of feeling.

Then, abruptly, Atlas produced a long, wicked-looking knife; it must have been concealed somewhere in his clothes. With knife in one hand and Indian club in the other, he moved forward, driving Phelps into the center of the room. Evading Atlas' first lunge with the knife, Phelps fell on his back, so that he was gazing straight up at the ceiling from which dangled the trapeze. Atlas leaped on him, but with a quick thrust of his trained feet, Jim flung him aside and leaped up.

The advantage was only momentary. Jim had lost his only weapon in the fall and Atlas was advancing once more, knife in hand. There was only one way to go—up. Phelps sprang straight upward, clutched the bar of the trapeze and swung clear by inches of Atlas' slashing knife. On the return swing, he timed his move carefully and struck Atlas full in the face with both feet. The man went flying in one direction, his knife in the other. It was a powerfully stunning blow—more than enough to kayo a heavyweight fighter of champion rank.

Jim Phelps leaped down and moved in to secure his prisoner, who lay motionless on the floor. But Atlas came back with a karate chop that narrowly missed the key spot. Jim, sitting atop the prostrate spy, took no further chances. He delivered three crushing right-hand punches to the man's jaw. Then, from the cuff of his trousers he drew a miniature hypodermic needle which he inserted in the large vein of the man's right arm. Then, with a sense of propriety rare in a man of James Phelps' profession, he retrieved Atlas' discarded nose from the floor and put it back in place as best he could.

Then he borrowed one of his captive's cigarets and settled back for a well-earned breather.

It was not to be. Phelps was startled by a sudden pounding on the door, followed swiftly by the opening of the door and the sound of heavy footsteps. Jim rose, shakily, and got ready once more for the worst.

# CHAPTER 12

The ponderous footsteps, as it turned out, belonged to Willy Armitage. Jim Phelps wasn't an emotional man, so he wouldn't contemplate kissing the powerful I.M.F. operative on both cheeks in the Gallic manner. But he was ready to give him the *Croix de Guerre* right on the spot.

"Willy, how in the devil did you track me down?"

"Us humble porters have our grapevine. We keep in close touch with the elevator operators—and they know *everything*. Who's the body on the floor?"

"That, Willy, is the object of our search. None other than the man named Atlas."

"So all our problems are over. All we do is put him on a plane and ship him special delivery to the good old U.S."

Phelps shook his head. "No can do. This guy is

red-hot contraband. And Mr. X, the big agent from Mao-land is after him too. He'd never get out alive."

"So what happens?" Willy scratched his massive head in puzzlement. Although he was a master at executing any job assigned him, long-range planning wasn't his strong point.

"What happens is, we first figure out how to get him out of here quickly before we're detected—and then find a place to hide him. Now let's see." Phelps' eyes scanned the room as he brainstormed the problem. "Yes . . . yes, this should do it. Listen. Jim Phelps wants to do some exercises—but not with the common herd. He wants an exercise mat in his room."

"So?" Willy didn't quite get the drift.

"So, who takes the exercise mat up to Mr. Phelps' room and stashes it in the extra closet? Who else but Willy Armitage, the porter. And who's inside the exercise mat sleeping like a baby?"

"—Our friend, Atlas?"

"Right. Only one thing: *you* implement the plan. I'm tired. I've got a headache and a sore arm and I'm going to lie down and put some ice cubes on the places that hurt."

Twelve minutes later the broad-backed figure of porter Willy Armitage was seen going up the freight elevator, a large canvas mat balanced nonchalantly on one shoulder. This was an unusual mat, since its total weight was over 200 pounds. But it wasn't noticeable, for Willy Armitage had most unusual shoulders.

Jim Phelps, in dressing gown, lay on his bed, feeling considerably better. He had showered, rested and licked his wounds. There was a tall glass of scotch and soda by his side, and it looked as though he was going to live a whole lot longer than he had thought he would about an hour ago. He'd sent a message via Willy to Mabel Moon apologizing for having left her party so early. Within that message was a coded message. It instructed her to contact all members of the I.M. Force and inform them that Phase Four of Operation Judas was now to begin, and also to give them the number of the alternative plan to be put in effect.

Jim looked over toward the closet where the object of the mission was stashed. The powerful dosage injected in Atlas' veins was good for sixteen hours. With reasonable luck, they should have the spy on a plane for Kennedy International Airport in New York well before that.

Phelps had to remind himself, however, that this was the trickiest and perhaps the most dangerous part of the operation. With the spy "on ice," as it were, it was very hard to avoid complacency. But complacency was the deadliest enemy of the secret agent. *The moment you let up, even for a split second,* Jim told himself, *bad things start happening to you.*

Jim Phelps got up from the bed and walked over to the open window. Below, lit by spotlights, was the red, white and blue canopy of the American Bar. He could hear the tinkle of a piano, a high, clear voice singing indistinguishable words, and then the sound of applause rising through the night. He thought about Mabel Moon; right now he supposed she was enjoying the applause. Most people did. Jim Phelps himself could never understand it; he was a man perfectly adapted to his chosen profession, a man satisfied to do his work in total anonymity, satisfied just in knowing that he'd done the job he'd set out to do. He glanced again toward the closet where Atlas lay in drugged silence. *That* was his satisfaction, and that was more than enough for operative James Phelps.

Feeling a warm glow after the last wave of applause, Mabel Moon walked back into her dressing room. Barry Coker shoved his head in the door.

"You were fine tonight, sweetie, just f-i-n-e. How d'ya feel about joining me for a dip in the pool before bedtime?"

"No thanks, Barry," she said. "I'm weary. But listen, return this pen to that nice Mr. Olson. He's out in the audience tonight and he wants to have a nightcap with me, but I just can't face it."

"Sure, tootsie, I'll make your apologies," said Barry Coker. As Mabel handed him the pen—and a scrawled note for himself—the fun-loving mask of the musician slipped for a moment. Partner with him in danger, Cinnamon Carter saw the serious face of secret agent Barney Collier. Both of them, she thought to herself, loved the excitement of the game. But sometimes the strain began to take its toll. Barney waved a cheery goodbye and left.

Speaking of the strain taking its toll—Mabel leaned toward the image of herself in the mirror as she removed the make-up from her face. She squinted one eye, then the other. She thought she had spotted a new wrinkle earlier this evening. Now, happily, she couldn't locate it.

Mabel was looking forward to the luxury of a long sleep. Atlas was captured and she had done her part, relaying instructions to "Coker" and "Olson" on Phase Four of the mission. There *was* one big problem as far as she was concerned: if they were to wrap up the operation today or tomorrow, she'd have to think of some graceful way of breaking her commitment to the American Bar. She had promised that nice Mr. Henreid that she'd stay over for another week.

Make-up removed, she slipped out of her evening gown and into a simple, blue street dress. She then sat down at her dressing table to give her hair two hundred strokes with the brush. It was a ritual she performed faithfully every night of her life, no matter how tired she might be.

She was interrupted by a light tapping at her door.

"Come in," she called.

The man who entered was a slender, long-faced waiter she couldn't remember having seen before. He carried a plate with a white envelope on it. "Message for Mam'selle," he said.

She took the envelope and extracted the letter. It was in a wretched scrawl. Studying it closely she made out that the sender would be complimented if Miss Moon would join him at his table in fifteen minutes for a late supper. The signature was illegible.

Mabel turned toward the waiter, shaking her head vigorously. "No, not tonight. Please give the gentleman my apologies. . . ."

There was an odd look on the waiter's face. She became aware then that someone else had noiselessly entered the room. A large hand was suddenly clamped over her mouth. A handkerchief with a strong, sickening scent was placed over her nose. She felt herself dizzy, swooning. She fought for what seemed like endless time. Actually, it was only a matter of seconds. As the darkness swept over her, she felt herself being lifted up and carried in powerful arms. And then she knew nothing more.

# CHAPTER 13

The note reached James Phelps just as he'd turned off the light and made ready to go to sleep. His arm was sore as the devil, and he cursed the knocking at the door. Curtly, he tipped the messenger and grabbed the note off the tray, slamming the door as he did.

The note was short, sweet and to the point. It read:

You have something we want—the man. We have something you want—the lady. Exchange to be made this coming morning at 5:00 at Ship Warehouse 7, Quai Gustav Ador. Do not come early. We will not be there. Any tricks and lady is kaput.

There was no signature. Jim rang Cinnamon's suite and got no answer; he didn't really expect one. These boys didn't fool around. This was for real. Swiftly, he started getting into his working clothes. There were a dozen things to be done, and all must be done immediately. Willy must be notified, told to bring in Barney and Rollin Hand for an emergency meeting. A safe place for that meeting had to be chosen—it couldn't be here. And someone had to be assigned to protect the priceless cargo in Jim Phelps' closet.

He reached Willy at the night porter's station and gave him the word to pass on to Barney Collier and Rollin. They were all to meet—as if by accident—in the lobby in thirty minutes. It wasn't by any means an ideal conference room. But its very openness gave it a certain cloak of innocence.

Jim stalked up and down the room. Now there was nothing to do but wait . . . and think . . . and worry. He was well aware that what he was about to do broke a number of cardinal rules in the Impossible Missions Force book. Primary was the fact that the success of the mission meant everything, individuals meant nothing. If the mission was accomplished and none of the team came back —success. If the mission was stymied and everybody came back alive and healthy—failure. That was the only way the faceless boys in the Secretary's office looked at it. Those were the terms on which Phelps and Rollin and Barney and Willy —and Cinnamon Carter—had signed. That was what they were all honor-bound to live by.

Jim sighed. It all made sense, logic. He had the Big Score locked up in his closet. He could forget about this new "problem," smuggle Atlas aboard a jet and go home a hero. Except—Barney and Willy and Rollin would never speak to him again.

And, for that matter, Jim Phelps would never speak to *himself* again. And that would ruin his value to the I.M.F.—and probably ruin the other boys too. There was his rationalization. *This* was why they had to pull a certain long-legged, blonde-haired chestnut out of the fire. Not because of loyalty, affection or any of the rest of that sentimental guck. Simply because, if they didn't, they'd be throwing away a million dollars' worth of talent. Jim revised his figure: no, make it two million.

He checked his watch. Time to go downstairs and meet his accomplices. He hooked up a special burglar alarm tied in with a minuscule receiver in his breast pocket, double-locked windows and the front door, then rode the elevator down whistling. He felt very good about the reasons he had come up with. They were a bit phony—but at least they were reasons for something his bones told him he had to do anyway. James Phelps was a great believer in what his bones told him.

In the lobby Willy, the night porter, met him: "Mr. Phelps, there are a couple of gents looking for you."

"Thanks, Willy. You don't have to join in. Your job on this one is to guard the merchandise upstairs."

Willy nodded respectfully and retired to the night porter's cage.

Jim found Rollin Hand sitting coolly on a divan in the very center of the lobby. He gave Hand a warm, banker's "Howdy" and then led him over to where Barney Collier was studying a display of paper-back novels in the now locked-up smoke shop.

"Mr. Olson, I'd like you to meet a young man whose music I've been enjoying a lot during my stay here. Plays a lot of piano at the American Bar. What's more, he's an American."

The slim young Negro nodded distantly toward "Olson", and turned toward the banker, waiting for an introduction.

"Oh, Oscar Olson, meet Mr. Barry . . . Mr. Barry . . ."

"Coker, Mr. . . ."

"Jim Phelps is the name. And touché, Mr. Coker. Now why don't the three of us Yankees go somewhere around this place and have us a drink?"

The English Lounge was vacant and ready to close, but a ten-dollar bill persuaded the lone bartender to pour three double Scotches on the rocks. In five minutes, Phelps sketched out the problem.

"We're going to have to improvise. But since we're dealing with a ship warehouse, Barney, you'd better bring your underwater demolition kit. And you, Rollin, you'd better get your make-up kit out tonight if you're going to look like Mr. Atlas tomorrow morning. And if things don't go right tomorrow, your nose is on its own!"

For the sake of appearances, the three fellow Americans lingered ten minutes longer, carrying on a heated discussion of the merits, respectively of the American vs. National League, with special reference on Phelps' part as to how the Boston

Red Sox would have triumphed over the St. Louis Cardinals had he been the Sox manager during the late, lamented series. Then they broke up and went off in different directions. The die was cast.

All the way down the Quai Gustav Ador, with Rollin Hand in the back of the rented Microbus, wrapped authentically in an exercise mat, Jim Phelps kept saying to himself, *Think of something clever, Think of something clever.* But somehow, for perhaps the first time in his life, the old brain didn't function creatively.

Then, as they pulled up at Ship Warehouse Number 7, a new thought lit up in James Phelps' mind: subconsciously, they expect us to pursue an intricate Oriental course of negotiation—being Orientals themselves. But suppose we fool them —just come on strong with vigorous, Yankee action involving direct tactics. *I understand you're holding our girl captive. . . . Take that . . . Splat! . . . Whap! . . . BAM!*

Realistically, Jim Phelps knew that this wouldn't work. Modern methods were the key.

"Barney, you have the right tools for this problem. Rollin and I will distract 'em as long as we can. You figure out some smart way to blow them to Kingdom Come—without ruffling Cinnamon's hair."

Barney Collier nodded as he jumped off the bus, half a block from its destination. With him he carried seventy-five pounds of equipment, mostly underwater, including enough explosive charge to blow half of Geneva into the lake of the same name.

Ship Warehouse Number 7 was a long, ramshackle, gray building, reaching out into the lake for over forty feet. Phelps parked the Microbus directly in front of a double door, in which stood a stocky man with a boxer's face. In his hands the man held a machine pistol which, Phelps estimated, could slice him completely in half within ten seconds.

Jim had, subconsciously, expected a bunch of funny, mixed-up little Orientals in pigtails running around saying "Mittah Pherps" and "Ah, so!" What he got instead was a cool, Occidental-gangster approach.

"Bring your prisoner inside the warehouse," grated the stocky fellow with the pistol.

Jim Phelps, after a struggle, managed to get the mat containing Rollin Hand slung over his shoulder. Staggering, he navigated inside the door of the warehouse and dumped his substantial burden against the nearest wall.

The stocky man wasted no time in preliminaries. "We must, of course, examine the merchandise to make sure it is sound—and *authentic*."

"The same applies in my case," said Phelps. "You must produce Miss Mabel Moon in healthy condition or our negotiation must end."

The thug with the gun gestured to two men in sailor suits, who stood at attention on the slick-looking, forty-foot motor cruiser docked inside the "warehouse." Going below decks, they brought up a stretcher in which was strapped a pale-looking but obviously alive Mabel Moon. She flapped a hand weakly at the sight of Jim Phelps, but clearly she was under some kind of sedation, in no condition to help herself.

"All right, Mr. Phelps, it's time to exhibit your specimen," growled the blunt-faced man with the machine pistol.

Slowly, hesitantly, Jim untied the cords binding the exercise mat containing his only trump card—Mr. Rollin Hand, actor and *farceur extraordinaire*.

The stocky man and his thin-faced lieutenant examined the pasty face of the man inside the exercise mat. "He seems larger than the Atlas we'd been led to expect," said the second-in-command.

"Give him the *nose test*," grumbled the boss man with the machine pistol.

The lieutenant advanced cautiously and studied the face of the purported spy Atlas. Then he reached out and squeezed the nose of the prisoner. Despite the surprising vigor of the squeeze, the victim showed no sign of emotion.

There were several other preliminary tests, but Jim Phelps knew that the ultimate test was coming. It came, when the chief of the Other Side said in guttural tones, "Now, Mr. Atlas, please show us how your nose comes off."

This was a critical moment for Rollin Hand, thought Phelps. All his legendary poise would be needed to delay this dread instant of reckoning. And, he thought, it was also a testing time for Barney Collier. Could the boy mechanical genius perform the impossible—rescue Cinnamon Carter from her toils and dispose of the blunt-faced head man and his minions at the same time?

As Rollin Hand seized his nose and, seemingly, removed it in toto before the stunned eyes of the man with the machine pistol, a block and tackle suspended from the ceiling of the boathouse suddenly lifted a long, narrow object out of the pleasure cruiser anchored at the dock. Jim Phelps, out of the corner of his eye, saw that it was the stretcher containing the supple form of Cinnamon Carter. Now she hung helplessly from the ceiling. But there was no time for contemplation. Mysterious sounds were heard from underwater.

"Now, Jim," came a cry from somewhere under the dock. Carried away with enthusiasm, Phelps recovered some of his old football player's skill and with Hand's help threw a few savage blocks that hurled the Chief of the Other Side and his friends onto the foredeck of the cruiser. At the same time the boat burst loose from its moorings and, with an explosive roar, surged backward, out of the boathouse.

The cruiser had barely cleared the outer extremities of Warehouse Number 7 when there was a convulsive roar; chunks of timber flew in every direction. Running out on the dock surrounding the warehouse, Jim Phelps saw that the once admirable cruiser had been blown into a pack of driftwood. Returning to the interior of the warehouse, he saw Mr. Barney Collier carefully lowering the stretcher containing Cinnamon Carter into a small dinghy.

114

They hoisted the stretcher onto the dock and unstrapped Miss Carter from her bonds. She lay there, helpless. "I think somebody's going to have to carry me," she said. "My arms and legs seem to have gone to sleep."

"The devil with your arms and legs," retorted the dramatic Mr. Rollin Hand. "I think my nose is broken. If *it* goes, there goes my beauty."

Barney Collier patted Mr. Hand and escorted him to the Microbus. It was James Phelps who bent down, took Cinnamon Carter up in his arms and carried her tenderly to the waiting vehicle.

Everybody agreed, as they drove back toward the Mont-Blanc, that it had been a most exciting dawn.

## CHAPTER 14

It was the afternoon after the Big Explosion.
Mabel Moon (known to some as Cinnamon Carter) spent most of her morning sleeping. A little
before noon, she had a half grapefruit sent up to
her room, along with a pot of black coffee (no
cream).

Her arms and legs were still sore from being
tied up so long. And the sickening scent of chloro-
form still lingered in her head. Moreover, she had
a painful interview coming up with Mr. Erich
Henreid—that charming man—in which she had
to break her word and tell him that she couldn't
keep her commitment to appear at the American
Bar for another week.

Most of Cinnamon Carter was quite simply Cinnamon Carter, girl spy, she thought, half flippantly
and half reverently. Yet there was another, frac-
tional part of herself if that would always and
forever, from now on, be Mabel Moon. It was a

corny and silly role, and she didn't kid herself about the quality of her voice or her future in "show business." Yet, there was something real and genuine that had gone into the part she'd played so briefly. *Yeah,* she thought to herself, *Mabel Moon lives. Oh, yeah.*

And why does Mabel still live, she asked herself. The answer was, she replied, because people like Barney Collier and Rollin Hand had stuck their necks out, risked their own lives to bring her back for encores. And then, there was that fellow Jim Phelps. A real grouch, but what a group to have around when the game was getting sticky. Cinnamon Carter knew well that Phelps and the rest of them had risked the success of the whole bloody mission to rescue Mabel, or rather, Cinnamon—or maybe both. In any case, she thought as she picked at her half grapefruit, she would work out some way to thank everybody properly one of these days. She started humming very softly to herself. . . .

Barney Collier was a slim, silent guy who sometimes got depressed, had what he called "black feelings." Very often, he'd say to himself—and sometimes to his good friends—"Why not? I'm in a lousy business." One of those good friends was a man named Jim Phelps. Another was Rollin Hand. And another was that lovely chick, Cinnamon. And Willy Armitage, he wasn't so bad, even though he didn't do much *communicating.*

Barney got a great deal of support from *knowing.* The sure feeling when he spliced in a circuit, diagrammed a complex electrical problem, solved a really tough equation, wrestled with higher calculus and pinned the whole thing to the mat. Mostly, he got a kick when *his* contribution to the I.M.F. team got somebody *off* the hook. For instance, what got him out of those "black" moods was seeing the expression around Cinnamon Carter's mouth when he got a line tied to the stretcher yesterday and yanked her right out of the hands of those creeps who were ready to wipe out her life.

Barney Collier didn't like the word "technician." It made a man something less than human. And, dammit, the only thing that mattered in the long run was to be *human*, to have human feelings. Everything else, including the jobs he did for the I.M. Force were, he liked to think, small contributions to *being human*. If he stopped thinking that, he'd probably throw up the whole damn business. Barney Collier was fairly sure his colleagues on the I.M. Force felt pretty much the same way. O.K., sometimes you did some unpleasant things. But you wouldn't touch them with a ten-foot pole unless they led to something better. A better world, with no "black feelings" in it— or at least not very often. Yeah.


Willy Armitage thought to himself: I'm helpful when big things have to be carried around. Or when something valuable has to be guarded so it won't get away or be stolen. Good old Willy. Strong as a horse. And willing. Not stupid either, mind you. Comes up with ideas quite often.

But still, he thought, with a touch of bitterness, *a workhorse*. That was the word somebody high up in the echelons above the I.M. Force had used in describing Willy. So, he thought to himself, maybe I should have been the ninety-seven-pound weakling. Maybe I shouldn't have built myself up physically, gone into the Olympics, wrestled at college, done all those physical things. Maybe I should have been an actor. Or a singer. Or an electronic nut.

Then the essential Willy Armitage came through. He looked out his bedroom window and saw a beautiful morning. Sun shining; everybody in the Force safe and sound. Mission accomplished —almost. Willy was basically a man who took life as it was. He was content—yes, more than content —with the job he did. And that was why he did it so supremely well. Willy had no complaint against life. Or the world. Or the people in it. He liked things the way they were. And particularly this morning. Wasn't it going to be a beautiful day!


Rollin Hand had a hangover and a nose that wouldn't stop hurting. He had given a lot of himself to the people in his group. ("I only regret that I have but one nose to give to my country.") He saw himself now in the role of Nathan Hale, standing nobly erect, the noose around his neck.

This is the problem for me, said Rollin to himself. Most people go through life playing just one part. Me, there's something chemical inside me,

I've got to play a gang of them. And the worst part of it is, I'm expected to excel in all of them.

Somewhere back in high school, Rollin Hand recalled learning that a common housefly has a hundred—or is it a thousand?—eyes. That's the way it is with me, he mused. Being by nature and inclination an actor (not necessarily in the Broadway or Hollywood sense) I have to look at the world through a thousand eyes, understand it from a thousand different viewpoints.

Understand, Rollin said to himself, I don't mind the danger or the bad hours or the evil companions I sometimes run into. But I do wish I could find one part—just one part—I could really get hold of, sink my teeth into, hang onto for a decent period of time. What an actor really needs for happiness is a nice long run in a juicy part. And what you get in this I.M.F. outfit is short runs all the time. One day I'm Jack the Ripper, next day I'm No-Nose Atlas. It's too bad I'm so sensitive. Why can't I be more of an every-day, run-of-the-mill guy. Like, say, Jim Phelps. If I were more like Jim, thought Rollin, I wouldn't have this sore nose and this blasted hangover.


Jim Phelps sat in bed, envying all his comrades. Right now, they were all sleeping the morning away, while he, the leader, was saddled with the problem of worrying about the delicate Phase Four of Operation Judas. . . . Some people had all the luck, thought Phelps, rolling over and falling sound asleep.

# CHAPTER 15

Jim Phelps woke up around 1:00 P.M. and the hotel had sent up the afternoon papers. Big head-lines described "Mysterious Boat Explosion on Lake." No bodies found, but apparently everybody aboard had perished. There was no mention of any discoveries that might lead the authorities to think the blow-up was anything other than an acci-dent.

Phelps was in a fine mood. He had had some solid sleep. His bruised arm had stopped hurting. He had checked his "patient" Atlas early in the morning when he'd returned from the warehouse. Pulse and respiration were normal. He had fed him intra-venously, then given him another shot to keep him under for an additional sixteen hours. The sun was shining. Everything was moving. It was time to set Phase Four in motion.

He lifted up the phone and asked for Miss Mabel

Moon's suite. There was a long wait, and then a drowsy, languorous voice said, "Hellooo."

"Miss Moon? This is Jim Phelps," said the caller. "I'm sorry if I disturbed you, but I have something to tell you. I'm a rich, old admirer of yours and I'm going to give you a present I think you're going to like."

"An anteater?" inquired Mabel, with a faint note of sarcasm in her voice.

"No. Even better than that," said Phelps. "Since you can't seem to guess, I'll tell you. A brand-new Swiss concert grand piano."

"Oh, swell," said Mabel. "Just the thing to carry in my purse when I go to parties."

From this response, Mr. Phelps could tell that Miss Moon didn't really comprehend the magnitude of his gift. Taking this in his stride, he set about making arrangements for delivery of the piano to the airport. He was on the phone for the next couple of hours, explaining that his own technician, Mr. Collier, had to check the instrument out before delivery to the airport, and hence it must be brought up to his suite immediately.

By four o'clock in the afternoon, three sweating workmen had delivered a monstrous crate at Phelps' door. An hour later, Mr. Phelps called downstairs, asking that the strongest porter in the place be sent up to transport the magnificent gift to the airport.

At 5:57 P.M., Mr. Willy Armitage entered a freight elevator on the 11th floor, wheeling a case of monster proportions. Three quarters of an hour later, he wheeled it out of a van and into the area marked "Customs" at the Geneva Airport.

Sitting coolly in a chair, long legs crossed, was the well-known singer, Mabel Moon. She'd been getting along famously with the customs inspector and his assistants right up to this moment. But when the hulking Armitage brought in the immense crate, the assistants began buzzing like bees, and the inspector knotted his handsome black eyebrows in a frown.

"You realize, of course, Miss Moon, that this object can't go through unopened. We must *inspect* any boxed object over a certain size. I won't bother you with the precise details of the regulations involved."

Barry Coker, the slim Negro pianist in a Carnaby Street jacket and trousers had remained in the background until now, humming softly to himself. But now he stepped forward in protest.

"But, man, you don't get the *idea*. What we have here is a musical instrument of the highest *class*. You take it out of that case, you going to jeopardize international relations. Could even cause some kind of international incident."

The inspector was unimpressed with Barry Coker's arguments. He insisted on inspecting the grand piano. And so, Willy Armitage was directed to open the case.

When the slats were removed from one end and Armitage gingerly eased the piano out of its protective cover, Barry Coker's boyish face lit up with pleasure.

"Man, that is a *machine*," he enthused.

The inspector's flunkies were twittering around the great piano, but it was the Inspector himself who insisted on lifting the lid.

"You're going to let me give you a quick concert, right, man?" said Barry Coker. It was more of a statement than a question. The slim young man plumped himself down on a packing case and commenced caressing the keys without further ado. What came out were a highly original series of variations on the old favorite, *Going Home*. The inspector, who professed to like opera but who really dug jazz, gave up trying to peer inside the works after the first few bars and sat on the corner of a desk, toes tapping and eyes gleaming behind silver-rimmed glasses.

As the music ended, the inspector gave the signal for the instrument to be recrated. This was done without misadventure. However, one curious event took place as Mabel Moon, Barry Coker and the piano were approaching the plane that would take them to Kennedy Airport.

Barry Coker stroked the crate housing the piano and said, sotto voce, "O.K., Atlas, baby, the theme is *going home* and the tempo is supersonic."

# EPILOGUE

Jim Phelps was still at the Hotel Mont-Blanc two days later. His bags were packed and checked into the airport, but there were still a few banking chores to do. After all, a man had to do some kind of justice to his cover occupation.

Willy Armitage had gone home the same day as Cinnamon and Barney, on a later flight. Rollin Hand had stayed over until yesterday—some emotional complication with that hefty redhead with the funny German name.

Now James Phelps was in the great city of Geneva by himself. Here was an opportunity to savor the delights of the place, but even the great Fodor's guide couldn't lure him. He was, after all, a faceless man—a man without emotional ties either to places or to people.

As he stood at the mail desk preparing to leave, there was a gentle tug at his arm.

"Mr. Phelps—Jim. Do you remember me, Lara Bergquist? How long are you staying? Perhaps you can show me a little of the city?"

It was the big, beautiful Swedish blonde he'd met in Paris.

Jim Phelps, bird of passage, decided he might stay a few days longer.